# The Cruise of the Rolling Junk

# The Cruise of the Rolling Junk

F. Scott Fitzgerald

Published by Hesperus Press Limited
19 Bulstrode Street, London W1U 2JN
www.hesperuspress.com

Foreword © 2011 Paul Theroux
Introduction © 2011 Julian Evans

Designed and typeset by Fraser Muggeridge studio
Printed and bound by CPI Group (UK) Ltd, Croydon CRO 4YY

ISBN: 978-1-84391-462-4

# Contents

# Foreword

This jaunt, an eight-day trip by car from Connecticut to Alabama, seems the merest merry footnote to F. Scott Fitzgerald's history, and yet...

Both literary and personal, it is a telling footnote, for what it reveals of his character, and the way it shows how he converted his life into his fictions. He believed this travel piece to be important; he rewrote it extensively, and had hopes for it. He also needed the money. The trip occurred at perhaps the happiest period in a life that was hectic, often sad, and at times tragic. It is, among other things, the excursion of two reckless, posturing and self-conscious people, 'possibly', as one biographer wrote, 'as a holiday from their honeymoon'. Scott and Zelda got married in April 1920. They set out on this trip three months later. They were a golden couple. For Fitzgerald it was a period of elation; his first book had recently been published and was a success; he was newly married to a lively southern girl – he was twenty-three, she was nineteen.

'We were about the most envied couple in America around 1921,' Scott said, in a conversation that was recorded in the 1930s.[1]

'I guess so – we were awfully good showmen,' Zelda replied.

'We were awfully happy,' Scott said.

Ten years after the trip described in 'The Cruise of the Rolling Junk', writing from a clinic in Switzerland where she was recovering from a nervous breakdown, Zelda reminisced in a tone of melancholy sweetness about the long-ago pleasure.

'We bought the Marmon with Harvey Firestone and went South through the haunted swamps of Virginia, the red clay hills of Georgia, the sweet rutted creek bottoms of Alabama. We drank corn on the wings of an aeroplane in the moonlight and danced at the country club and came back, I had a pink dress that floated and a very theatrical silver one...'[2] But at the time of the trip she had written to a friend saying that 'The joys of motoring are more or less fictional.'

Although 'The Cruise' is not a long piece, it is composed of many different tones and uneven in its elements, fact mingled with fiction – and the fiction is not half so memorable as the fact. In its bravado and occasional silliness, it is an attempt to capture the spirit of the age that Fitzgerald defined in his novels and stories of the period – impulsive, foolhardy, bibulous and free-spending. It is, as well, an oblique portrait of America, mostly rural and homely, wounded by war.

Fitzgerald depicts the car they used for the trip as a character with a distinct personality: handsome, lovable, unreliable, fast one minute, stalled the next. Fitzgerald's own pose is that of a klutz who has no mechanical aptitude, as well as a reputation (borne out by this piece) as a very poor driver. He revelled in his amateurishness. His car, a 1918 Marmon, was built by the Nordyke Marmon Company in Indianapolis. He had bought it second-hand at the time of his marriage. It was a model known as Speedster, accommodating two passengers, with six cylinders, spoked wheels, and capable (as Fitzgerald proves) of travelling at 70 mph. In 'The Cruise' he calls it an 'Expenso', and for its defects, 'The Rolling Junk'.

The piece is one of the first in that most American of narratives – a tradition in American travelling and travel writing – the long road trip by car. It is now so familiar a subject as to be hackneyed or old hat for the holiday pages of a newspaper, but for anyone who has ever driven through America, even today, it is an unfolding delight. Twenty-five years after Fitzgerald, Henry Miller crossed the country in his old Packard for *The Air Conditioned Nightmare*. In 1960, John Steinbeck rode around the U.S. in a converted pick-up truck for *Travels with Charley*, and in the same spirit, William Least-Heat Moon sought out back roads in *Blue Highways* in a van he called 'Ghost Dancing'. In each of these trips, the car is a character, more meaningful and lovable to the writer, perhaps, than to the reader, to whom this anthropomorphism cannot but feel cute.

The conceit of Fitzgerald's trip is that it is a quest, in this frivolous case for the biscuits and peaches that were unobtainable to the southerner Zelda in her new home in the north. No sooner has Zelda expressed a craving for them than Scott says they must leave immediately: 'Seating ourselves in the front seat we will drive from here to Montgomery Alabama, where we will eat biscuits and peaches.'

They are soon on the road. It's a happy idea, but like much in the piece it was probably prettified for the sake of exuberance. They did not leave from their home in Westport, but from New York. This is a quibble, though. 'The Cruise' is specific when it refers to the overnight stops they made, which after New York were: Princeton; Washington, DC; Richmond, Virginia; Clarksville, Virginia; Greensboro, North Carolina; Spartansburg, South Carolina; Athens, Georgia; and finally Montgomery, Alabama, 1,200 miles in eight days.

The piece deploys what became standard effects in road trip literature, the shifting gears of high hopes, disappointing reverses, sudden landscapes, brief encounters, breakdowns, and changes in tone. Fitzgerald is on familiar ground in the north, especially in the stop at Princeton, where he had been a student only a few years earlier. He does not let on that he has been this way before, many times, as a soldier stationed in Alabama (where he first met Zelda), and on numerous train journeys from New York to Montgomery over several years when he was courting her. Zelda is better able to judge the south, and, as a southern coquette, knows how to appear helpless and to flirt in order to get help. The prevailing theme of the piece is that they are innocents, and a bit too stylishly dressed for this region; victims of the road and its perils, of the car's eccentricities, of weather and delay and the shortage of money. This last item, at any rate, was a serious obstacle. Fitzgerald, a spender, who was in debt for most of his life, wired his friend Edmund Wilson for money while he was on the road: '*Touring South. Shy of money.*'

In 1920, the Civil War was still a powerful memory. Many of the older people whom the Fitzgeralds encountered would have had hideous recollections of the bloody battles, either from family history or direct experience. This Fitzgerald makes clear after Fredericksburg where 'a garrulous gasoline dispenser told us that his father had participated in the battle'. And later that day: 'At sunset we plunged into the Wilderness – the Wilderness where slain boys from Illinois and Tennessee and the cities of the gulf still slept in the marshes and the wooded swamps – but over the bloody ground there was only the drone of the cicadas now and the sway of the lush vines.'

But, epitomising the egotism of the age, instead of listening to any eyewitnesses to the war, Fitzgerald saw himself and his own exploits as central to his trip. He was not travelling to listen but rather in the thrust of exhibitionism. This is the chief weakness of 'The Cruise'. The south was still wounded, still bleeding. Some of his most heartfelt descriptions in the piece concern the war and the landscape but there are too few of them. Even his mentions of the Great War, two years in the past, are mere throwaways, as of a fleeting glimpse of a veteran in Washington: 'He was a young man, a returned soldier, still wearing part of his uniform.'

Fitzgerald was a perfectionist in his work, one of the most serious and dedicated of writers; and he could be brilliant, as he shows in *The Great Gatsby* and *Tender is the Night* and many stories. Though he did not live long – he died at the age of forty-four – at the end of his life he had learned to be sober, uxorious, and punctual. This was a side he did not show to his public until 1936 when he wrote the magazine pieces gathered together as *The Crack-Up*. Until that melancholy and powerful confession he had always been known as breezy. Breeziness was his mode of living, as well as his journalistic style.

What is apparent, and painful, in 'The Cruise' is that Fitzgerald's attitude towards black Americans is unforgivably breezy to the point of pure ignorance. There are a number of demeaning references in this piece to blacks. One of Fitzgerald's biographers, Jeffrey Meyers, has shown how Fitzgerald's attitude changed from fashionable anti-Semitism in the 1920s to sympathy with Jews during the rise of Nazism, as evidenced in his portrayal of Monroe Stahr in *The Last Tycoon*.[3] But Fitzgerald never corrected his negative bias against blacks. It is obvious from his work and his life that he did not know any blacks, and as Meyers shows in his biography, Fitzgerald was himself déclassé and socially insecure. Meyers says, 'Princeton intensified his comforting sense of superiority, and he confirmed the beliefs of readers of popular magazines.'

The trip, taken on impulse, took two years for Fitzgerald to process. In 1922, he set to work, and wrote 'The Cruise of the Rolling Junk' from notes he had made. He left out the longueurs, he brightened it with afterthoughts, he coloured it with fictions. It is not entirely accurate, yet it is full of wonderful touches, as when they arrive at the outskirts of Montgomery:

> We spoke little now. When automobiles passed we craned our necks looking for familiar faces. Suddenly Zelda was crying because things were the same and yet were not the same. It was for her faithlessness she wept and for the faithlessness of time. Then into the ever-changing picture swam the little city crouching under its trees for shelter from the heat...

At the end of 'The Cruise' the couple find Zelda's house in Montgomery empty – irony of ironies, her parents have left to visit her in the north. This wasn't true. In fact, they were away, but not far away, and the Fitzgeralds lived it up (as Zelda wrote from the clinic) until they returned.

It was two years after taking the trip, in June 1922, that Fitzgerald wrote to his agent Harold Ober, 'I've sent you... a 25,000 word touring serial, humorous throughout, for the [*Saturday Evening*] *Post*. I think they could run it as a 3 part thing in which case it'd be nice to get $2500 for it...'4 But the *Post* turned it down. Fitzgerald offered to cut it to fit the magazine. They remained uninterested. Fitzgerald wrote to his agent: 'It was quite a blow...' He suggested sending it to *Scribner's Magazine*, but guessed he might not earn more than $500 for such a sale. He mentions the possibility of other magazines, and months later, 'What has become of *The Rolling Junk*?' Still later, 'Any dope on *The Rolling Junk*?'; 'I spent a month of The Rolling Junk + while I realize that technicccally [sic] it isn't a success still I should hate to let it go for two hundred dollars.'

Four years after the trip, 'The Cruise of the Rolling Junk' appeared in three instalments in the monthly magazine, *Motoring*. In a serious examination of 'The Cruise', the Canadian scholar Janet Lewis writes that it is 'prophetic not only of the fiction that Fitzgerald was to write, but of the direction the Fitzgeralds' loves would take. The spontaneous actions, the inability to cope with practical matters, the eccentric behaviour so amusing in [The Cruise] and so much a part of the Fitzgeralds' personal charm would lead to their future unhappiness.'5

*– Paul Theroux, 2011*

# Introduction

I first came across 'The Cruise of the Rolling Junk' when I was researching a radio programme for the BBC in 1996. It was the year of its author's centenary. Remarkably, given that he was the author of *The Great Gatsby*, a book that belongs as much to American mythology as American literature, that radio show was, as I remember, the only marking of the anniversary in the British media. Its title was 'The Authority of Failure': the phrase was F. Scott Fitzgerald's, contrasting himself with his friend Ernest Hemingway in one of his Notebooks – Ernest, who always spoke 'with the authority of success. We could never sit across the table again.' Then again, perhaps that title reveals one of the reasons for Fitzgerald's neglect. It is somehow appropriate that a writer whose life has accumulated at least as much mythical status as his best-known novel should at the same time be ignored, on account of his wholesale embrace of failure. Such is the present's permanent nervousness about the lasting quality of its own success.

What did Fitzgerald's failure consist of? 'All in three days I got married and the presses were pounding out *This Side of Paradise* like they pound out extras in the movies,' he wrote. Two years earlier, in 1918, he had fallen in love with the baby-faced Zelda Sayre; a year later she had ditched him. This sort of reverse was familiar to his adolescent, confused, aspirational and over-eager personality: through school, Princeton and the army he had become habituated to disappointment. Then abruptly, in the autumn of 1919, the New York publisher Scribner's reversed his fortunes again by accepting his first novel. On the strength of it he got the girl back, and in April 1920, at the age of twenty-three, he was published and married. His dreams had come true.

Yet at exactly the same moment, the romantic in Fitzgerald was profoundly frustrated by the loss of his dreams. In an obscure way, what he could lose through fulfilment and success came to mean more to him than what he could gain. Through the alcoholic years of the Twenties, the ashtray-throwing years on the French Riviera, the years of '1,000 parties and no work', the squandering years when he and Zelda constantly outran spectacular earnings from his writing, it was to those pre-success days that he reverted. 'Once in the middle Twenties,' he wrote,

> I was driving along the High Corniche road through the twilight with the whole French Riviera twinkling on the sea below. As far ahead as I could see was Monte Carlo... It was not Monte Carlo I was looking at. It was back into the mind of the young man with cardboard soles who had walked the streets of New York. I was him again – for an instant I had the good fortune to share his dreams, I who had no more dreams of my own.

In an essay called 'Those Wrecked by Success' Sigmund Freud writes how surprising and bewildering it at first seems when 'one makes the discovery that people occasionally fall ill precisely when a deeply rooted and long-cherished wish has come to fulfilment'. At the pathological level, that is what Fitzgerald's life after the publication of *This Side of Paradise* and marriage to Zelda feels like: an incurable illness whose symptoms were alcoholism, waste, collapse and attempted self-destruction. As if, having made his dreams of success come true, he had nothing with which to replace the yearning that had been satisfied – except another yearning, to throw the success away.

Fitzgerald was semi-consciously aware of his pathology. In 1936, in the autobiographical piece I quoted above, he wrote of his early success as a burden as well as a bonus, something that came with a 'compensation' – as though he experienced it as an encumbrance. The compensation, he said, was that he stayed young 'in the best sense', and had 'fair years to waste, years that I can't honestly regret, in seeking the eternal Carnival by the Sea'. The acknowledgement here is more important than the lack of regret: it doesn't seem to have been in Fitzgerald's nature to regret very much.

But this picture is not wholly true or complete. The waste happened – the gaudy spree that mirrored America's own, the inability to apply himself to work, the summers spent permanently drunk, the vulgarity of having to make a scene whenever he entered a room – he tested most of his relationships to destruction, and finally his marriage crashed too and Zelda with it, within months of Wall Street's crash, as if the two had the same source. Yet as a writer, as opposed to a drunk, an exhibitionist or a husband, he lived carefully and honestly from the material he provided himself with. His literary conscience stayed sober. In J.B. Priestley's introduction to the first British edition of Fitzgerald's collected works,[6] Priestley is right to say that Fitzgerald 'was considered an alcoholic hack by writers who never possessed and could hardly begin to understand his fine artistic conscience, his sense of obligation to his talent. He was a wild drunk who never yet ceased to regard himself and his doings with astonishing detachment and truthfulness.' In *The Best Times* John Dos Passos, who met Scott and Zelda in 1922, identified them as celebrities 'in the Sunday supplement sense' but nevertheless paid homage to Scott. 'When he talked about writing his mind, which seemed to me full of preposterous notions about most things, became clear and hard as a diamond. He didn't look at landscape, he had no taste for food or wine or painting, little ear for music except for the most rudimentary popular songs, but about writing he was a born professional. Everything he said was worth listening to.' Both these judgements suggest that there was an unviolated core to the writer, despite his personal failure, and even that his outward failure was a bulwark, a way of protecting his most important asset: his talent.

What I found most remarkable about 'The Cruise of the Rolling Junk', as soon as I read it, was how much of the fulfilled future this purposely lightweight account – a serial in three parts based on a journey he and Zelda made just after *This Side of Paradise* appeared and he was at the zenith of success – portends. The impression was so strong that the story seemed not to have been written shortly after the journey, but retrospectively by several decades, looking way back into Fitzgerald's past – it was as though I were reading a confirmation of his trajectory from a much later date, or that this is how his life would have started if it was going to turn out the way it did: as if he were a character made up by a novelist named Fitzgerald.

With Fitzgerald's novels there is often a temptation to read them as autobiographical. With 'The Cruise of the Rolling Junk' there is the opposite temptation, to read it as wholehearted fiction. The sense of reading a story or a novella rather than a true account is heightened by his dramatisation (you might as well say melodramatisation) of events and the narrative's Wodehousian echoes. It's in no sense an exercise in reportage, or in style or reflection: it was intended for one of the big-circulation magazines to which he often sold stories. Yet its frivolity derives an uncanny truthfulness from the accuracy with which it reverberates with presages of the writer's life to come.

It was not an easy sell. Fitzgerald wrote the story up in spring 1922, two years after the event, just after the publication of *The Beautiful and Damned*, his second novel. His agent sent it to the *Saturday Evening Post* but the *Post* declined it, and Fitzgerald worked on it some more until it was eventually sold to *Motor* magazine for a pretty miserly $300. It was published in three parts in February, March, and April 1924, by which time he was working on *The Great Gatsby*. The dates, the delay, the story's extended genesis as a narrative all suggest that Fitzgerald may also have felt there was something determining about it.

'The sun, which had been tapping for an hour at my closed lids, pounded suddenly on my eyes with broad, hot hammers.' When the story opens, the Fitzgeralds had been living the life of Connecticut aristocracy for two months, having quit New York and its permanent liquid revelry to write (Scott) and read and swim (Zelda). Their first establishment as husband and wife at the eighteenth-century farmhouse they rented at Westport became fraught almost immediately, with Scott trying to work and the nineteen-year-old Zelda jealous of his absences and vexed by his control over her life. With the start of the house-party season, the household went downhill fast. The July Fourth weekend, the house crammed with Scott's Princeton friends, continued from Sunday through to Thursday, when the party was wrapped up by one of the guests calling the fire brigade. (Legend has it that when firefighters asked where the fire was, Zelda pointed to her breast and said, 'Here!') Fitzgerald had to reimburse the town for the cost of the hoax. At the weekend the party restarted, and so it is possible that the couple's decision to leave Westport four days later, on the 15th, was not so whimsical as his published account suggests; it may have contained a motive of desperation.

Fitzgerald's announced reason for the journey – a 1,200-mile dash from Westport to Montgomery, Alabama, where Zelda had grown up, to fetch her the southern peaches and biscuits for breakfast that she craved – frames the story as a lark, a romantic refusal of reality. 'To be young, to be bound for the far hills, to be going where happiness hung from a tree, a ring to be tilted for, a bright garland to be won – It was still a realizable thing, we thought, still a harbor from the dullness and the tears and disillusion of all the stationary world.'

It is also a dare, in which he and his wife comically pit their nerves and endurance against each other. The competitive state of the Fitzgeralds' relationship is the first thing the reader learns about their life together. As soon as Scott wakes up he finds Zelda in his room, 'singing aloud. Now when Zelda sings soft I like to listen, but when she sings loud I sing loud too in self-protection.' Their rivalry is intense. Moments later, when the 'wild idea' of the journey comes to him and 'parade[s] its glittering self around', he is satisfied to see that she is properly impressed. The reflex to outdo each other grows into a leitmotif that reaches a climax when their car throws a back wheel outside Baltimore. In the aftermath of finding help and fixing the wheel back on, Scott demands to know why Zelda was bent double with mirth in the passenger seat after the wheel went bowling past them. '"I had more fun than you did"', she shrieks '"and that's what we came for".'

The intensity of these skirmishes interests us, I think, because of Fitzgerald's ability to draw comic energy from them, and because they are also the story of an absence – Fitzgerald describes few countervailing tendernesses between the couple as they romp and wriggle egotistically towards their destination. His studied exploitation of their competitiveness might then reasonably be construed as an indicator of his private view of his marriage – as might the ledger he kept through his working life, where each year he summarised for himself what kind of a year it had been. At the end of 1922 his judgement was harsh: 'comfortable but dangerous and deteriorating, no ground under our feet'.

The heart of the comedy is located in the Fitzgeralds' automobile. The roads of the 1920s were mainly unmetalled, and a distance that would be routine in a modern car was an epic undertaking. (An advertisement in one of the issues of *Motor* in which Fitzgerald's account was serialised offers after-market Gruss air-springs with the slogan, 'Make all Roads Boulevards!') The Fitzgeralds' car was inevitably flashy and immodest. Fitzgerald nicknamed it an Expenso: in reality it was a Marmon 34, a swanky touring car with a racing pedigree. But the Fitzgeralds' Marmon had been bought second-hand and passed its prime, with what sounds like a badly welded chassis (Zelda having driven it over a fire hydrant in Westport) and many secondary defects, though still 'in a nerve-wracking and rickety way exceedingly fast'. Where the car was concerned, Fitzgerald cast himself in the role of sucker rather than incompetent:

Of course, while nominally engaged in being an Expenso, it was, unofficially, a Rolling Junk, and in this second capacity it was a car that we have often bought. About once every five years some of the manufacturers put out a Rolling Junk, and their salesmen come immediately to us because they know that we are the sort of people to whom Rolling Junks should be sold.

He certainly knew nothing about how cars worked. His skill with them was literary. Here the Rolling Junk is literally the vehicle for the narrative; elsewhere he was one of the earliest novelists to understand the significance of the new world of the automobile (as later in *The Last Tycoon* the aeroplane), and how it would change life, sexual relations and literature. One thinks straight away of the importance and underlined newness of the auto-mobile in the plot of *The Great Gatsby*, of the 'new red gas-pumps [that] sat out in pools of light' and the '"Big yellow car. New... going faster'n forty"' at the scene of Myrtle Wilson's death.

According to Fitzgerald's account of the trip to Montgomery, he and Zelda set out within half an hour of the idea being born. Twelve hundred miles rich in disaster follow: every particular of auto-related calamity – meaningless signposts, importunate darkness, grave-deep ruts, wrong-way streets, blow-outs, a spare tyre called Lazarus, shed wheels and batteries, pompous guide-books, a map-reading wife, highwaymen, thunderstorms and sandstorms, derisive onlookers, know-it-all motorists – happens (though actual mechanical breakdown is rare). Misfortunes often draw crowds and are then related in the style of a conversation of the early Twenties, one wisecrack after another ('Cracks had to fly back and forth continually like the birds in badminton,' Dos Passos remembered): as at the outset when the couple are doing no more than filling up with gasoline:

'You mean to say you're going somewhere in this Rolling Junk that it takes a week to get to?'

'You heard me say Alabama, didn't you?'

'Yeah. But I thought that was the name of a hotel up to New York.'

Somebody in the crowd began to snicker.

'Which half the car you going in?' demanded an obnoxious voice, 'the high half or the low half?'

'Race you there in Schneider's milk wagon.'

'What you goin' to do, coast down?'

The atmosphere was growing oppressive.

The wisecracking is, as it usually is, an outer shell of comedy paying tribute to latent disaster, but something deeper is going on here too, that will reach from this adventure into the rest of Fitzgerald's life. Beneath the couple's competitiveness and badinage (lost near Princeton, '"We can camp out," proposed Zelda dreamily. "An excellent idea," I agreed. "I can turn the car upside down and we can sleep under it"'), they radiate an uncomfortable impression that they have dangerously few resources between them, not just to keep them going down the hurrying yellow ribbons of road toward the south, but to stay together at all. The comedy also hints at Fitzgerald's alcoholism ('In Westport we stopped at our favorite garage and were filled with the usual liquids, gasoline, water and oil of juniper – or no! I was thinking of something else') and a running gag about running out of funds has them, for a punchline, crashing the North/South Carolina toll bridge without paying and reminding us that a decade later they themselves would crash, with profounder consequences.

Not that one minds, in a way – as one of those onlookers – because one suspects, in fact one is certain, that the moment Fitzgerald takes a step towards being less reckless he'll probably start to become less interesting as a writer. But the greatest portent is still to come in the shape of the couple's welcome at Montgomery, as they at last roll down Dexter Avenue, Zelda weeping 'for the faithlessness of time', for how things are the same yet not the same, and the little city 'crouching under its trees for shelter from the heat'. Arriving, they find the house of Judge and Mrs Sayre shuttered and locked. The lady next door calls over, 'Why, Zelda, child, did you ride down here in an automobile?', and in Fitzgerald's reaction to her explanation, that the judge and his wife have themselves left for Connecticut to surprise the couple, he releases all the ironic fulfilment to which their adventure is pledged.

'Ah, and it was bitter how well they had succeeded!'

Even though his version is not strictly true (Zelda's parents did not travel up to Westport until August), Fitzgerald is expressing the greater shape of his conviction: that personal surprises will blow up in his face; things must end badly, or at least heavily qualified; the path of life winds towards disillusion; and failure is his condition. He must break things, and break things up. On that, you might say, he cannot be faulted. The genuine romantic intuits that they cannot be allowed to achieve their goal, that it can only be approached close enough to shatter it, for the elementary reason that, having once achieved it, there no longer remains a quest to live for.

On the way to such a willed and fulfilled failure, and within the limitations of the quest, a large space – the space of poetry – is nevertheless opened up where a lyrical sensibility can work and, as it will turn out, transcend the irony of those limits. Soon Fitzgerald will publish *The Great Gatsby*, the novel Harold Bloom has called his 'Keatsian' version of the quest. In 'The Cruise of the Rolling Junk' there are already descriptive passages, between the wisecracking and the frippery, that are both gorgeous and mature: not landscapes or cityscapes or crowds and certainly not individuals, but vistas, perspectives and, above all, lighting. It has been said that Fitzgerald wrote for the movies without knowing it, and it's impossible not to notice here the way everything is lit, as it will be in *Gatsby*. This is the couple's first view of Virginia:

A cool wind blew, faint and fresh. Slow short hills climbed in green tranquility toward a childish sky. And already there were ante-bellum landscapes – featuring crazy cabins inhabited by blue-black gentlemen and their ladies in red-checked calico. The south now – its breath was warm upon us. The trees no longer exfloreated in wild haste, as though they feared that October was already scurrying over the calendar – their branches gestured with the faintly tired hauteur of a fine lady's hand. The sun was at home here, touching with affection the shattered ruins of once lovely things. Still, after fifty years we could see the chimneys and wall corners that marked the sites of old mansions – which we peopled with pleasant ghosts. Here under the gay wistaria life at its mellowest had once flourished – not as on Long Island with streets and haste and poverty and pain just twenty miles away, but in a limitless empire whose radius was the distance a good horse could travel in a morning and whose law was moulded only of courtesy and prejudice and flame.

Yes, of course there is sentiment here too (there's also patronising dismissiveness towards blacks, dismayingly not the only instance of it); but the wistfulness is there because the writer desires the domesticated sun, the loveliness and extent of the view to shift and falter in the last line, precisely so that they can be regarded in the next paragraph under differently angled light that reveals not just Virginia's picturesqueness but its 'selfconscious insistence on this picturesqueness' in its cherishing of 'its anachronisms and survivals, its legend of heroism in defeat', and the 'tinny and blatant' quality of its soul. This is the perspective-changing by which the poet begins to remake reality, to engender and assert the value of his subject, and Fitzgerald will use it lavishly in *The Great Gatsby*: specifically in, say, the eroticism of Daisy's sudden stormy tears as she admires Gatsby's soft, rich piled-up shirts or in Nick Carraway's shouted compliment in the wake of Gatsby's confession,[7] and more generally in our changing views of Nick as well-mannered friend and then prig or of Daisy as an unhappy beauty and later unforgivably careless woman. Many things – I'm tempted to say everything – in Fitzgerald's universe seem to predicate their converse, not least ideas of success, hope, and destiny.

'The Cruise of the Rolling Junk' turns out to contain other foretastes of *Gatsby*. For one thing, the Fitzgeralds' destination is not just an ante-bellum but, as he makes clear, a prelapsarian America, and their journey is not just into the south but into the past: an impossible return, as Gatsby's is. Both pieces of work nurse an equation of balmy summer and automobile travel, and there are reused details: the Rolling Junk's wheel falling off and associated reactions to it; a character who steps out into the road when Zelda is driving; her accelerating (as Daisy Buchanan does) rather than braking. Rhythms of prose remind us of later, refined rhythms: 'We rested only five minutes – there was sunshine all around us now – we must make haste to go on, go down, into the warmth, into the dusky mellow softness, into the green heart of the Alabama town where Zelda was born.'

Forgotten, even assumed dead years before he died in 1940, then rediscovered in the 1950s, Fitzgerald has continued to be viewed by a curious, puritanical in a class-burdened way, consensus as a lovely but not a serious writer: as though, at worst, he was a snob and a suck around the rich, or at best that his belonging to the finite flashy myths of the Jazz Age excludes him from consideration. Yet as he said in 1940, when someone repeated the charge that he fawned on the rich, 'I always thought my progress was in the other direction'; and if he ever was superficial, then the complex honesty and humanity of his superficialities has turned out to offer a harder, truer portrait of the American century than the mysticism and pose-ridden individualism of many of his contemporaries and successors.

This may be difficult to grasp when contemplating a description of one of Gatsby's West Egg parties, or when studying Fitzgerald's own dissolution. It is certainly impossible to grasp if you consider truth, or writing, to be utilitarian matters. If Fitzgerald were alive today and, looking for readers, decided to write a blog containing his writing tips for aspiring novelists, how much of a fan base would he accumulate if, instead of explaining how to introduce characters, generate plot or use impact words, he quoted Keats on the necessity of serving Mammon, extolled the value of failure, and asserted the importance of a life thrown away on a dream?

Should we feel like catching hold better of Fitzgerald's durability and achievement, or putting a more complete description to his work than 'lovely', we might take another route and make an effort to get at what lay behind his embrace of failure – to go back in time from 1920 rather than forwards. It tends to be forgotten, because he emerged in the all but deafening early Twenties, that he was a post-First World War writer not a pre-Second World War writer, and that he was, albeit at a distance (because he did not get to France), a casualty of that war and a member of a generation that, faced with a vacuum, expected too much too soon. Another way of looking at his situation might be that the war had cleft him and his contemporaries into a divided youth, one that possessed not only great innocence and willingness of heart, not to mention hedonistic energy, but also the mind of a lost and failed civilisation.

If so, then at one level at least, the philosophical one, Fitzgerald's life and writing are about how to live post-war, post-loss. He understood something else too: that the post-war world was continuing to use a failed civilisation as its model, that it was continuing to live in, as he describes it in *Tender is the Night*, 'the broken universe of the war's ending', and so his novels and stories, for all their vibrancy and charm, are, like the sometimes relentless wisecracking in 'The Cruise of the Rolling Junk', dramatisations of the coping strategies of an era that was, beneath its febrility, heartbroken and despairing. He wrote about exactly this when he was working on *Gatsby* in

1924: 'That's the whole burden of this novel – the loss of those illusions that give such color to the world so that you don't care whether things are true or false as long as they partake of the magical glory.'

'Show me a hero and I will write you a tragedy,' he wrote in one of his notebooks. His own mind, far from being a playboy's or a wastrel's, was that of an ascetic chronicling not just his failure but the massive faltering of humanity. That is what he means when, on the last page of *Gatsby*, he writes that Nick Carraway, sprawled on the beach, 'became aware of the old island here that flowered once for Dutch sailors' eyes – a fresh, green breast of the new world. Its vanished trees, the trees that had made way for Gatsby's house, had once pandered in whispers to the last and greatest of all human dreams; for a transitory enchanted moment man must have held his breath in the presence of this continent...'

'Gatsby believed in the green light,' we read a few lines further on, 'the orgastic future that year by year recedes before us'; but it is at the end of 'The Cruise of the Rolling Junk', in its final flash of premonitory knowledge, that Fitzgerald first sets out Gatsby's ideal, and our unappeasable hunger to return to a past from which to pursue it all over again.

'And yet – I have discovered in myself of late a tendency to buy great maps and pore over them, to inquire in garages as to the state of roads; sometimes, just before I go to sleep, distant Meccas come shining through my dreams... My affection goes with you, Rolling Junk – with you and with all the faded trappings that have brightened my youth and glittered with hope or promise on the roads I have travelled – roads that stretch on still, less white, less glamorous, under the stars and the thunder and the recurrent inevitable sun.'

*– Julian Evans, 2011*

# The Cruise of the Rolling Junk

# Part One

I

The sun, which had been tapping for an hour at my closed lids, pounded suddenly on my eyes with broad, hot hammers. The room became crowded with light and the fading frivolities on the wall paper mourned the florid triumph of the noon. I awoke into Connecticut and a normal world.

Zelda was up. This was obvious, for in a moment she came into my room singing aloud. Now when Zelda sings soft I like to listen, but when she sings loud I sing loud too in self-protection. So we began to sing a song about biscuits. The song related how down in Alabama all the good people ate biscuits for breakfast, which made them very beautiful and pleasant and happy, while up in Connecticut all the people ate bacon and eggs and toast, which made them very cross and bored and miserable – especially if they happened to have been brought up on biscuits.

So finally the song ended and I inquired whether she had asked the cook–

'Oh, she doesn't even know what a biscuit is,' interrupted Zelda plaintively, 'and I wish I could have some peaches anyhow.'

Then a wild idea came to me and paraded its glittering self around.

'I will ·dress,' I said in a hushed voice, 'and we will go downstairs and get in our car, which I note was left in the yard last night as it happened to be your turn to put it away and you were too busy. Seating ourselves in the front seat we will drive from here to Montgomery, Alabama, where we will eat biscuits and peaches.'

I discovered to my satisfaction that she was properly impressed. But she only stared at me, fascinated, and said, 'We can't. The car won't go that far. And besides we oughtn't to.'

I perceived that these were mere formalities.

'Biscuits,' I said suggestively. 'Peaches! Pink and yellow, luscious–'

'Don't! Oh, don't!'

'Warm sunshine. We can surprise your father and mother. We can just not write that we're coming, and then, one week from today we can just roll up to their front door and say that we couldn't find anything to eat up in Connecticut, so we thought we'd drop down and get some bis–'

'Would it be good?' begged Zelda, demanding imaginative encouragement.

I began to draw an ethereal picture – of how we would roll southward along the glittering boulevards of many cities, then, by way of quiet lanes and fragrant hollows whose honeysuckle branches would ruffle our hair with white sweet fingers, into red and dusty-colored country towns, where quaint fresh flappers in wide straw lids would watch our triumphant passage with wondering eyes...

'Yes,' she objected sorrowfully, 'if it wasn't for the *car*.' And so we arrive at the Rolling Junk.

The Rolling Junk was born during the spring of 1918. It was of the haughty make known as the Expenso, and during its infancy had sold for something over thirty-five hundred dollars. Of course, while nominally engaged in being an Expenso, it was, unofficially, a Rolling Junk, and in this second capacity it was a car that we have often bought. About once every five years some of the manufacturers put out a Rolling Junk, and their salesmen come immediately to us because they know that we are the sort of people to whom Rolling Junks should be sold.

Now this particular Rolling Junk had passed its prime before it came into our hands. To be specific, it had a broken back-bone unsuccessfully reset, and the resultant spinal trouble gave it a rakish list to one side; it suffered also from various chronic stomach disorders and from astigmatism in both lamps. However, in a nerve-wracking and rickety way it was exceedingly fast.

As to its appendages, it had been so careless about itself as to dispense with all tools except a decrepit jack and a wrench which upon proper application could effect the substitution of one wheel with tire attached for one wheel with tire blown out or punctured.

But to offset these weaknesses, which amounted to general debility, it *was* an Expenso, with the name on a little plate in front, and this was a proud business. Zelda was hesitating. She became depressed. She sat on the side of my bed and made some disparaging remarks about the cost of such a trip and about leaving the house for so long. Finally she got up and went away without any comment and presently I heard the sound of a suitcase being dragged out from under a bed.

And that's the way it started. Within half an hour after the birth of the Idea we were ambling along a Connecticut country road under the July sunshine. Three large grips crunched in the back seat, and Zelda's hand clutched in a four-inch map of the United States torn from the circular of the 'More Power Grain and Seed Co.' This, together with the two mournful tools and a pair of goggles with the glass out of one eye, was our equipment for the trip.

In Westport we stopped at our favorite garage and were filled with the usual liquids, gasoline, water and oil of juniper – or no! I was thinking of something else. During this process a number of individuals noted the suitcases and clustered about the car, and in nonchalant tones we explained to the dispenser of liquids that we were touring to Alabama.

'My golly!' exclaimed one of the onlookers in an awed voice, 'that's way down in Virginia, ain't it?'

'No' I said coldly, 'it's not.'

'It's a state,' said Zelda, giving him what might be termed a mean look. 'I come from it.'

The geographic person was subdued.

'Well,' said the garage man cheerfully, 'you going to stay all night there, I see.'

He pointed to the bags.

'All night!' I cried passionately. 'Why, it takes a week to get there.'

The garage man was so startled that he dropped the filling pipe and the gasoline flowed over his shoes.

'You mean to say you're going somewhere in this Rolling Junk that it takes a week to get to?'

'You heard me say Alabama, didn't you?'

'Yeah. But I thought that was the name of a hotel up to New York.'

Somebody in the crowd began to snicker.

'Which half the car you going in?' demanded an obnoxious voice, 'the high half or the low half?'

'Race you there in Schneider's milk wagon.'

'What you goin' to do, coast down?'

The atmosphere was growing oppressive. I was sorry we hadn't said merely that we were running down the post road to New York. We had difficulty in being properly haughty when the garage man, who had been consulting physician to the Rolling Junk for several months, looked at us with his head shaking solemnly and remarked in a funereal tone:

'God help you!'

I threw the gear lever into first.

'Don't worry!' I said sharply.

'You better have a hearse body put on.'

I took my foot off the clutch, intending to shoot away from this distasteful scene with a triumphant rush, mowing down, if possible, several of the rapidly swelling throng. Unfortunately the Rolling Junk chose this moment to give a little sneeze and doze off.

'That car knows its business,' commented the garage man. 'This here "Alabama" talk is like asking an old man's home to get up a football team.'

By this time I had coaxed the engine into a loud erratic cackle, and with a great groan we sped away and went galloping down the post road to New York.

Now if I were Mr Burton Holmes I would describe in detail all the places we passed between Westport and New York – of how in one place the natives all wear blue hats and waistline suits, and how in another they wear no clothes at all, but spend their days swimming in the sunshine in an old mud-hole not more than a hundred yards from the road. These places you may find detailed in any automobile guide book with their pop, and their points of interest, together with how to jog left into and jog right out of them. You may take them for granted – the educational part of this article begins a little farther on.

There was a race course near New York, I remember, or perhaps it was an aerodrome, and there were many tall bridges leading somewhere, and then there was the city. Streets, crowds in the streets, a light wind blowing, the sunshine between tall buildings, faces splashing and eddying and swirling like the white tips of countless waves, and, over all, a great, warm murmur.

Enormous policemen with the features of Parnell, of De Valera, of Daniel O'Connell, gigantic policemen with the features of Mr Mutt, of Ed Wynn, of ex-President Taft, of Rodolph Valentino, grave features, roly-poly features, melancholy features, – all slid past us like blue mileposts, contracted and shortened, dropped far off, graduated themselves in a descending line like a sketch for a lesson in perspective. Then the city itself moved off, moved away from us and fell behind, and we, vibrating in involuntary unison with the Jersey ferry, were sorry for all the faces back there, could almost have wept for them, who could not taste the sunshine we were going to taste, nor eat the biscuits nor the peaches, nor follow the white roads from dawn to early moonlight … To be young, to be bound for the far hills, to be going where happiness hung from a tree, a ring to be tilted for, a bright garland to be won – It was still a realizable thing, we thought, still a harbor from the dullness and the tears and disillusion of all the stationary world.

## II

Across the river it was four o'clock. The marsh in which New Jersey floats glided by us, followed closely by the three ugliest cities in the world. We tore down a yellow ribbon of a road under one of those soft suns I had known so well for four years – suns that were meant to shine on the svelte tan beauty of tennis courts and on the green fairways of shining country clubs. Most of all they were the suns of Princeton, the white and gray and green and red town where youth and age nourish their respective illusions year upon lazy year.

We followed the yellow ribbon. The sun sliced itself into trigonometric figures, became a luminous cloud and was suddenly gone. Twilight came up out of New Brunswick, out of Deans, out of Kingston. Hamlets, nameless in the dark, turned yellow squares on us from scattered windows and then dark skies leaned over the road and the fields, and we were lost.

'Look for towers,' I said to Zelda. 'That'll be Princeton.'

'It's too dark.'

A sign passed us at a crossroads – stretched out the plaintive white arms of a ghost. We stopped and, dismounting, I struck a match. Four names stared momentarily out of the dark. One only was familiar – New York, 30 miles. This was a relief; at least we were still on our way *from* New York – or, depressing thought, perhaps *to* New York. At least we were not *in* New York, nor on the other side of it – though of this last fact I was not certain.

I turned to Zelda, who was placidly enjoying the set table of the sky.

'What'll we do?'

'Well,' she answered finally, 'we can't tell by the map of the More Power Seed Company, because all over this part of New Jersey it just has a big white circle that says, "More Power Seeds used exclusively in this section".'

'It's after nine o'clock.'

'Look at that moon,' she pointed avidly. 'It's the–'

'Yes, but we want to get to Princeton, and eat and sleep.'

'Do you mean to say that you went to Princeton for four years and don't know the names around here well enough to recognize places right near it?'

'For all I know, these villages may be near Atlantic City – sort of suburbs. Listen! By Golly, we *are* on the shore. Listen to the surf–'

Then we begun to laugh. The surf, if it was the surf, was mooing. In the dark, the heavy, velvet dark, we laughed aloud, and the cow with a grassy flourish and a kittenish kulump of her hoofs, galloped away to play ocean at the other end of the pasture. Then silence save for the steady lament of the Rolling Junk's motor and our voices that were still and small now, like well-behaved consciences.

'Do you really think' – her tone was sincerely curious – 'that we're near Atlantic City? If we are I'd like to go there.'

The cow mooed again, far away; the moon without any apology passed under a cloud. I re-entered the Rolling Junk and began to feel uneasy.

'We can camp out,' proposed Zelda dreamily.

'An excellent idea,' I agreed. 'I can turn the car upside down and we can sleep under it.'

'Or we can build here,' she suggested. 'You can take the tools and build a house. Or do you think you can build a house with only a tire wrench – but then you've got the Jack too–'

Zelda began to sing a hymn, hoping for Divine intervention. Then she gave up and began to sing the Memphis Blues. But the song had not the faintest effect on the implacable heavens, so we started down the road looking for a house. We decided that if we found one that did not have the unmistakable aspect of a criminal's den or of a place where a witch lived, we would stop and inquire our way. If the house we chose happened to be a hell-hole I would pretend that the tire-wrench was a revolver and soon bring the wretches to terms.

But we stopped at no house, for when we had gone a hundred yards we came to a stone bridge and beneath it there flowed a stream. The moon came out and there in silver tranquility the Stonybrook meandered along past its Corot elms. We were within a mile of Princeton. Over the bridge with a solemn rumble, past the Gothic boathouse with its dreams of faded Junes, up through a short rising wood into midsummer Princeton, asleep as surely as if General Mercer had still to writhe on its memorable hill under a British bayonet.

Nassau Street was desolate – it was too early for the tutoring schools to draw down their netfuls of the ambitious, the lazy, the dull – and the Nassau Inn was almost as dark as its haughty crony Nassau Hall across the street.

Entering I discovered the stout and cynical Louie behind the counter, Louie who trusts without believing. It is his tragedy to have seen his famous bar grow dark – a bar where Aaron Burr had sipped the wine of conspiracy, where ten generations of fathers and sons had reveled, and where now, alas, the walls, made of the carved tops of a hundred immemorial tables, will ring no more to the melodies of Rabelaisian song.

'O thou beyond surprise,' I said to Louie, 'give me a room and a bath for self and wife. We journey to the equator in quest of strange foods and would sleep once more beneath an Aryan roof before consorting with strange races of men such as the cotton-tailed Tasmanians and the pigmies.'

Louie knew me not, though he divined that I had once been of the elect. He agreed that I could have a room and whispered to me that town and college were quiet as the dead. We rolled to the garage, where the colored man in charge seemed, to my chagrin, to take our arrival quite as a matter of course. He actually told me that upon payment of a nominal sum I could leave the car there all night.

We returned, walking slowly under a gentle cheerful rain, to the Nassau Inn, and all night the quiet water fell on the blue slate roofs and the air was soft and damp.

## III

Then it was morning, and after the rain the grass on the college campus was very green. It was patterned grass, a lake very smooth and cool, and out of it gray castles rose softly to a low Gothic and faded out against the grayness of the sky. There were dozens of these granite islands in the great lakes of grass – some were poised upon terraces that were huge static waves, some were strung along in graceful isthmuses and peninsulas, weaving here and there, and joined up eventually to other peninsulas by bridge-like cloisters over the green, green water.

At nine-thirty, the sun leaned into sight above Nassau Hall and in the luxurious garage we inquired for the health of the Rolling Junk.

The garage man stared at it skeptically.

'How fah you goin'?'

I did not repeat the mistake I had made in Westport.

'To Washington.'

'Well,' he said slowly, 'you may make it, but I wouldn't bet you no good money on it–'

'There was nothing said about betting!' I retorted crisply.

'–because I never bet on no long shots like this-a-one. You may make it and then you may not.'

Upon receipt of this information, I stepped on the self-starter and the Rolling Junk filled the garage with a great roar and clamor. Then we were sailing down Nassau Street in the direction of Trenton.

Lawrenceville school's lazy red brick was asleep in the sun as we went past. We looked at the seed-catalogue map, but when we found that Trenton was covered by the legend about 'More Power Seeds' we tossed the map to a passing pig who was trotting briskly toward Princeton with the obvious intention of enrolling himself in the freshman class.

In Trenton we made our first horrible mistake. Having dispensed with the More Power Seed Map of the United States which, despite its hiatuses, did at least give us an idea of our direction, we purchased 'Dr. Jones's Guide Book for Autoists.' From that point onward the cadence of Dr. Jones's prose rang in our ears all day; the mysteries of his mileage, his knowledge of pop, and finally his ability to state all his conclusions forward or backward, were to us the powers of a demoniac spirit as infallible as the Pope.

To begin with, we referred to three indexes, and from their combined evidence we discovered that Philadelphia lay somewhere between New York and Washington – a fact which I had long suspected. This discovery was followed by a long search – 'Let *me* look.' 'Wait a minute – you've had it for hours.' ... 'I have not. If you'd just let me alone for a *minute!*'... 'Oh, all right, but you're not doing it like it *says*.' – until we made the further discovery that the first thing to do was to jog left along the turnpike.

'What does "jog" mean?' inquired Zelda.

'Jog? I think it means to put on all the gas and skid around the corners.'

She looked at me solemnly.

'I think it means to run in second.'

'What it really means,' I explained, 'is to turn round and round in big circles until we get out of a place.'

'Maybe it means to sort of bounce. How do we know a Rolling Junk *can* jog, anyhow? Maybe it takes a special kind of a car.'

Whether our course out of Trenton can be described as a jog or not, I do not know. Zelda held Dr Jones's Guide Book on her lap and gave me turning instructions as soon as – or at least almost immediately after – we reached each turning. Pretty soon the page which told how to get from Trenton to Philadelphia tore out and blew away, so we turned to the page which told how to get from Philadelphia to Trenton and read it backward, which did almost as well – almost, but not quite, because once we somehow got turned all the way around, and

started back toward Trenton. Then luckily, that page came out and blew away also, and we reached Philadelphia in the orthodox manner – that is, by inquiring the way from the sages who sit in front of country stores and are paid by the tire manufacturers to give wrong directions.

The day was still a callow youth when we entered the birth-place of Benjamin Franklin – or was it William Penn?

Just as we were disembarking from the car, a squad of police-men charged up and told us that this was a one-way street, but was liable to be changed to another-way street at any moment, in which case we would have to stand there until the following week, when it would be changed back to a one-way street again. So we drove up a mean-looking alley where there were no rules. There was a ragged individual hanging about, and as soon as I was able to catch his eye, which was so shifty as to be almost irretrievable, I told him that we were leaving valuable suitcases in the car and would be much obliged if he would tell anyone who came along not to take them. He said he would, so we walked away.

After luncheon we returned to the mean-looking alley. All was as we had left it except that the shifty-eyed man had disappeared. This was puzzling, but just as I was about to start the motor we heard a voice from a back window close by.

'Hey Mister,' the speaker's face was dark with hair and grime, 'you better set that old junk up to a stein of gasoline.'

We thought of course that this was merely more of that same ribald wit which seemed to be rife in Connecticut. But we were in error.

'Yes sir. She did you one good turn 'bout an hour ago.'

I scowled at him.

He leaned farther out of the window and the grime on his face shone enthusiastically as he talked.

'There was a bum with a mean eye snoppin' around her and he'd peek in at them satchels you got in there an' then he'd look up an' down the alley and then he stuck in his paw kind of slow when all of a sudden, *Bang!* – an' he give an awful jump and yelled out "Don't shoot!" an' tore up the alley like he thought the whole police force was after him.'

'Did you shoot a gun at him?' demanded Zelda.

'Not me. Your car there blew out a tire at him.'

I dismounted. Sure enough! The right rear tire was kneeling down.

'Did someone steal the tire?' enquired Zelda anxiously.

'No – it blew out. All the air came out.'

'Well, we've got another, haven't we?'

We did have another. Its name was Lazarus. It was scarred and shiny and had had innumerable operations upon its bladder. We used it only for running to the nearest garage whenever one of the other four was incapacitated. When we reached a garage our custom was to have the incapacitated tire repaired and re-placed, while Lazarus would be returned to his sleeping porch in the rear.

After twenty minutes I assembled the jack and elevated the groaning ruin four inches from the ground – Zelda meanwhile giving out such helpful texts as 'If you don't hurry we'll never get to Washington tonight,' and 'Why didn't you leave the jack under the rear seat so I wouldn't have to *move* every two minutes?' By the time I had replaced the blown-out tire by the wheel to which Lazarus was attached, she had become frightfully depressed.

At length we rolled cautiously out of the alley and began searching the neighborhood for a garage. A policeman gave us voluminous directions in terms of east and west, and on my assuring him that I had forgotten my compass he interpreted himself in terms of left and right. And so by and by we found ourselves in a strangely familiar locality, sounding our horn in front of a sign which read 'Bibelick's Family Garage.'

'Well, look what I see,' said Zelda in an awed voice. 'The alley back of this must be where we started from.'

For from the garage had stepped our late acquaintance, the man whose face was dark with hair and grime. 'Come back?' he growled cynically.

'You might have told us this was a garage,' I retorted with some heat.

Mr Bibelick eyed me pugnaciously.

'How'd I know you wanted a garage?'

'I want to get that tire repaired.'

'And we've got to hurry,' added Zelda', 'because we're going to—'

'Yes,' I interrupted hastily. 'We've got to get out in the suburbs right away. Just put a new tube in that casing and pump it up and put it on in back.'

After a gay spasm of cursing Mr Bibelick set to work. He took off the injured tire and contemptuously showed me a large hole I'd overlooked in the casing. I assented weakly to his assertion that I'd have to have a whole new tire. While he effected the necessary substitution Zelda and I amused ourselves by naming the rest of the tires. The two in front we called Sampson and Hercules, because of their comparative good health. The rear axle was guarded on the right by the aged Lazarus, covered with sores, and on the left by an affair of mulatto-colored rubber and uncertain age in which, nevertheless, we reposed considerable confidence. It was freckled but not bruised. I was for calling it Methuselah, but for some inscrutable reason Zelda named it Santa Claus. There was reserved for Santa Claus that very day an adventure so grotesque that, had we been granted premonition of it we would have named it something quite different.

The new tire affixed to the rear was designated as Daisy Ashford; at the same moment Mr Bibelick announced by a great burst of expectoration that his travail was at an end. By this time I felt that we had lived in Philadelphia for many days, that the Rolling Junk had become a house and would roll no longer and that we had best settle down and advertise for a cook and a maid.

'How about this old inner tube?' demanded Mr Bibelick scornfully. 'I'll throw it in back an' you can use it for a life-preserver if you get in any floods.'

'Don't bother,' retorted Zelda, who had become fidgety to an extent that would have delighted St Vitus. 'You can cut it up into oblongs and sell it for chewing gum.'

'Have I got water?' I asked.

Ostensibly answering me but obviously looking at Zelda, Mr Bibelick replied:

'You got plenty on the brain.'

The incredible cheapness of this repartee was revolting to both Zelda and me, so I started the motor and filled the air with smoky blue vapor. A little later we had left Philadelphia behind and still under a glittering sunshine, were running along the white roads of Delaware.

## IV

South across the Brandywine we wandered, along a plum-blossomed zigzag lined with copses white as snow. The sun fell west before us across freckled orchards. It hovered in the half sky, silhouetting, in gray against gold, ancient Dutch manor houses and stone barns that had been standing when Cornwallis, his black boots gleaming, came out of a crumbling town and yielded up an empire to a swollen posse of farmers – before that, when Braddock, the rash, died with a fashionable curse in a wood that was spitting flame. South we went – over little rivers and long gray bridges to placid Havre de Grace, a proud old lady with folded hands who whispered in faded dignity that she had once been under consideration for capital of the nation.

But she had married a plumber instead of a President and the fruit of the union was a large 'boomer' sign which swayed in blatant vulgarity over the street by which we entered, like a beggar holding out his cap for pennies.

Then through Maryland, loveliest of states, the white-fenced rolling land. This was the state of Charles Carroll of

Carrollton, of colonial Annapolis in its flowered brocades. Even now every field seemed to be the lawn of a manor, every village lane was a horse market that echoed with jokes from London coffee houses and the rich ring of spurs from St James Street – jokes and spurs more glamorous perhaps to the provincial beaux and belles for having reached them three months old. Here my great-grandfather's great-grandfather was born – and my father too on a farm near Rockville called Glenmary. And he sat on the front fence all one morning, when he was a little boy, watching the butternut battalions of Early stream by on their surprise attempt at Washington, the last great threat of the Confederacy.

On we traveled between woods lovelier than the blue woods of Minnesota in October when the mist is rising and fields as green and fresh as the fields of Princeton in May. We stopped at a little old inn, cobwebbed with climbing wild honeysuckle, and ordered an ice cream cone and a chicken sandwich. We rested only five minutes – there was sunshine all around us now – we must make haste to go on, go down, into the warmth, into the dusky mellow softness, into the green heart of the South to the Alabama town where Zelda was born.

From the Inn of Tranquility the roads were rare – an unbroken boulevard that made a broad band over high green hills and drooped symmetrically across sunny valleys. It was twilight before we turned into the pungent, niggery streets of Baltimore and early dusk when we set face toward Washington. The boulevard melted suddenly into a suburban street.

'Hasn't it been wonderful!' exclaimed Zelda happily.

'Wonderful. We've gone a hundred and eighty-one miles today. And yesterday we went only seventy-seven.'

'Gosh, we're smart!'

'And we've passed through six states and haven't had a bit of trouble – except that blow-out in Philadelphia.'

'It's the best thing that ever happened,' she said rapturously, 'and we've been outdoors and I feel wonderful and healthy and

– I'm so glad we came. How many more days before we'll get there?'

'Oh, about five – maybe four if we go awfully fast.'

'Can we?' she demanded. 'Oh, let's try tomorrow! All that stuff they said about the car was just silly. They were just trying to make us mad. Why–'

'Stop!' I cried fearfully. 'Stop–'

But it was too late. We had tempted fate with outrageous temerity – with a crash and a roar the drone of the world changed to thunder in my ears, the car seemed to fall to pieces before our eyes and it was as though we were flat on the street and being dragged, miraculously uninjured, between immense cobblestones which pounded and ground together as we went by. Yet we were *not* in the street – some relics of rationality told us that – we were on soft leather cushions and the wheel was still in my hand. In the instant of calamity some object had flashed by us at break-neck speed, something strange yet familiar, and then passed out of sight.

After an agonized and endless period of this crazy furious bumping – the car, or whatever piece of it we were still sitting in, was jerking frantically along at twenty miles an hour – I reached for the emergency brake, but, desperate as was the emergency, it refused to function. I knew at last that the whole rear end was dragging in the street. I heard Zelda make curious incoherent sounds beside me and I expected any second to be hoisted heavenward on a pillar of flame and offered up as a gasoline holocaust.

Then, it must have been two crimson minutes after the first wrench of the catastrophe, the Rolling Junk with a horrible leaping gesture came to a full stop.

'Get out!' I cried to Zelda. 'Get out! Quick! It's going to blow up!'

In the sudden quiet the fact that she neither moved nor answered, but only gave out that curious crying noise, seemed burdened with a sinister significance.

'Get out! Don't you understand? A wheel came off! We dragged! Get out!'

Suddenly my excitement changed to anger. She was laughing! She was roaring! She was bent double with uncontrollable mirth. I pushed her precipitately from the car and half dragged, half threatened her to a safe distance.

'Good God!' I stood there panting. 'The wheel came off! Don't you understand? The wheel – it's gone!'

'So I notice!' cried Zelda, rocking with laughter. 'It isn't there any more.'

I turned from her in frantic disgust. The Rolling Junk, trembling slightly, stood in ominous silence. Behind it a trail of sparks extended back for two hundred yards. More from nervousness than from intention I started off at a rickety dogtrot in the direction that the wheel and tire – it was Santa Claus – had taken. I suspected dimly that by this time it had reached the Capitol or had announced our thunderous arrival to the doorman at the New Willard. But I was wrong. Two blocks farther up I came upon Santa Claus, lying quietly on his side in an innocent slumber, apparently uninjured. Around him in the darkness were gathered a dozen children, staring first at the tire, then at the now starry sky, obviously under the impression that Santa Claus was a meteoric body fallen from Paradise.

I pushed my way with some importance through the group. 'See here,' I said, in a brisk efficient tone, 'that's mine!'

'Who said it ain't?' I think they suspected that I had been rolling it as a hoop.

'It came off,' I added, becoming rather sheepish as my excitement died. 'I'll take it with me.'

Hoisting it to my shoulder in as dignified a manner as is possible before young children, I staggered back the two blocks to the Rolling Junk, and found it surrounded by an enthusiastic crowd.

I joined Zelda and we stared with the rest. The car, its rear axle resting securely on the pavement, suggested a three-legged table. From all sides comments arose from the admiring Columbians, most of whom had been on nearby porches, enjoying the night in their shirt-sleeves.

'Wheel come off?'

'Gee! Lookit that there car!'

'Yeah. Wheel came off.'

'What happened? Wheel come off?'

'Yeah?'

'Where'sa wheel?'

'It come off.'

'It went up the street. You should of watched it go.'

'I seen it go. You should of watched. Gee!'

'I says to Morgan, "Well if I ain't a son-of-a-gun, look at that thing. It's a wheel," I says. An' Morgan says, "No," and I says, "Sure it's a wheel all by itself," I says.'

'What happened? It come off?'

'Yeah.'

'You'd of ought to seen the car go along. All of a sudden there was this noise and Violet and me looked and there was this car without no wheel, bumping along, an' the spark shootin' off behind like they was out of a skyrocket.'

'The lady in it was laughing.'

'Yes, I seen she was laughing.'

'She must of thought it was funny.'

By this time someone had noticed me, standing modestly, tire in hand, on the outskirts of the crowd, and a more reticent mood was communicated to the onlookers. Their remarks were now confined to asking whether the wheel had come off and I told them all politely that it had. They eyed me with suspicion. There seemed to be a vague feeling that in some way I had arranged it that the wheel should come off. We stood there chatting for some time. In fact, as the host I passed around a package of cigarettes. Several matches were struck and the axle was examined by all present. They exclaimed, 'Gee!' in the proper manner; one of them was kind enough to inspect the front of the car and even to try out the horn.

'The horn's all right anyhow,' said he – whereat we all laughed heartily, including me and excepting Zelda. She seemed to have done all her laughing in the stress of the catastrophe and I now perceived a dangerous light gathering in her eyes. She appeared to be measuring the distance between herself and the nearest onlooker.

'I think we ought to do something,' she suggested sternly.

'All right,' I agreed feebly. 'I'll go in a house and telephone for a garage.'

She continued her menacing silence.

'They can drag it into Washington, you see.' I turned to the crowd. 'I wonder if there's a telephone I can use.'

As though this were a prearranged signal, the crowd began to melt away. At least all of them who possessed telephones melted away, for when I repeated my question to the half dozen who remained they all answered either that they had no telephone or that they lived on the other side of the city. I was somewhat pained. It seemed to me that I had always granted the use of my telephone to castaways, even if they were strangers and it was after dark.

'Hey!' – One of the survivors was holding a lighted match to the axle – 'This thing's all right. I guess your brake-band's shot to hell for sure, but the axle's O.K. You can just jack it up and put the wheel back on.'

He was a young man, a returned soldier, still wearing part of his uniform. I was much encouraged. Anything mechanical from nail-hammering to applied dynamics is a great dark secret to me, and had this accident occurred in the center of the Sahara I would have walked to the Cairo garage before it would have occurred to me that the car could be patched up and driven on. Inspired by the young soldier and by another enthusiastic looker-on who immediately removed his coat, I made my usual search for the jack. Ten minutes later the Rolling Junk was assembled and so far as my inexpert eyes could determine, as good as new.

Grateful, but blundering, I took each man aside singly and attempted to 'at least pay you for your time,' but they would have none of it. The soldier turned me off easily – the other man, it seemed to me, was somewhat insulted.

'What on earth were you laughing at when the thing went blah?' I inquired of Zelda as we drove away, conservatively at five miles an hour.

She snickered reminiscently.

'Well – there was something about that crazy wheel shooting up the street and us bumping along and you with that silly expression on your face, tugging at the emergency and shouting something about going to blow up–'

'I saw nothing funny about it,' I retorted stiffly. 'Suppose *I* had laughed and *no*body had pulled on the emergency brake – where would we be now?'

'Probably just where we are.'

'We would not.'

'We would too. It just stopped of itself anyhow. That man said so.'

'What man?'

'That soldier.'

'When did he?'

'Back there. He said the emergency brake was automatically disconnected when the wheel came off. You might as well have laughed.'

'But I was right in principle anyhow.'

'But I had more fun than you did – and that's what we came for.'

Disheartened by this repudiation of my accomplishment, I drew up in front of the Willard, where a new problem immediately presented itself. Would they let us in? We – especially I – scarcely resembled the savory patrons catered to by fashionable hotels. The general effect I gave was of a black and tan ruin. My hands were two gray clots of oil and dirt, and my face was the face of a daring chimney sweep. Zelda too was draped with dust and according to her own feminine standards, infinitely less presentable than I. It took all our courage to leave the Rolling Junk under the door-porter's contemptuous eye and walk into the hotel. Walk? Rush is a better word. We tore across the lobby like pursued criminals, flung ourselves violently into the attention of a startled clerk and chattered out our apology.

'We've been turning – I mean touring,' I cried passionately. 'Turning down from Connecticut – I mean touring. We want a room and a bath. We've got to have one WITH A BATH !' I felt the need of impressing on him at once that we were not of the great unwashed, that from under these cocoons of dirt two gorgeous butterflies would presently emerge at the simple application of hot water.

He began to paw over a register. I felt that more pressure was necessary.

'My Expenso is outside – my EXPENSO!' I gave him time to associate the idea of incalculable wealth with the idea of an Expenso, and then I added, 'Is there a garage in Washington? I mean is there one near? Not in the hotel, I don't mean, but nearby? You see, my–'

He raised his head and regarded me dispassionately. I forced my face into a conciliatory smirk. Then he beckoned a bell-boy and we made ready for forcible expulsion. But when he spoke his words were like benediction.

'Twenty-one twenty-seven' he said without hysteria. 'Garage one block down and one over. They'll take any kind of a car.'

I leaned hastily over the counter and shook his hand.

# Part Two

Washington, as most Americans know, is generally considered the Capital of the United States. The population, including the diplomats from defunct governments, is estimated at – but as a matter of fact I believe it will be best to put the educational part of this article in a special appendix in the rear. I would much rather tell how we awoke in enthusiasm thinking that Virginia – the real south – was only an hour away. We ordered a gorgeous breakfast-in-bed – a joy dampened only by the news that peaches were unobtainable. Zelda, having never seen Washington before, had no desire to go sightseeing – for sightseeing is only a pleasure to those who can point and explain. However, the first public building I visited was the garage, where I went to inquire how the Rolling Junk had passed the night.

'Good morning,' said the garageman who bore an unmistakable resemblance to the late Czar of all the Russias. 'Is this your – car?'

I acknowledged it fearlessly. He shook his head more in sadness than in anger.

'If *I* was you,' the Czar suggested lugubriously, 'I'd get rid of it – if you *can*. If you can't, why you better lay up here a couple of weeks while I give her a thorough overhauling, put on new wheels and new tappets, get rid of some squeaks and groans, find some new lights, burn the carbon out of the cylinders, buy four new tires and send for another axle to put in for that bum one–'

'But she looks all right,' I said persuasively. 'All except that little list to the side.'

'Well,' said the Czar with melancholy despair, 'I had two men waitin' since seven o'clock. They been puttin' on new brakebands 'stead of the ones you wore off in your accident. Be ready 'bout four o'clock, maybe.'

'Four o'clock! I've got to get to Richmond by tonight.'

'Best we can do,' sighed the Czar. 'Your battery's wore out, too. It ain't had no water.'

'Oh, no. I can fix that.' And going up to the battery I gave it a violent shake. 'See?'

To his astonishment it now worked. Why, I do not know. When shaken at regular intervals it would resume its functions and behave itself for as long as a week at a time.

'Well, look at your wheels then. That one with the hunk of rubber on it. Or is that just some old cloth wound around the wheel?'

'That's Lazarus,' I suggested politely.

'Whatever it is. I thought it was a Goodstone Cord. Anyhow that wheel's only got a few good spokes left. Some day it's just goin' to collapse on you. It's like riding on an egg.'

He had me here. I seized the wheel and shook it violently as I had the battery, but there was no result. The spokes remained broken. He had me on the tappets too, but this was scarcely fair as I wasn't sure what a tappet was. The Czar explained that there were eight of them and that they held down an affair called the 'blotter'. If there had been thirty-two of them or even sixteen, it would have been all right – but this blotter was particularly wild and eight tappets wouldn't keep it down. I asked the Czar if he couldn't put eight more tappets on, but he said he wasn't in the manufacturing business.

Having done my best for the Rolling Junk I left the Czar to his gentle Romanoff melancholy and returned to the New Willard to find Zelda dressed and restless. I told her the lamentable news.

'Let's turn back,' she suggested immediately. 'We'll never get there. Never. We might as well turn back. Think of all the money we're spending. Seventy-five dollars yesterday. It'll be fifty dollars more before we get out of Washington and that'll leave us only eighty out of our two hundred.'

I explained that we had to get a new tire yesterday.

'But we'll probably have to get one every day. Lazarus is about to explode from old age and Santa Claus won't go another hundred miles.'

'But I'm going to have the bank wire us money to somewhere in South Carolina and then we'll be perfectly safe.'

Zelda, who is astonishingly naive, was amazed and cheered at the notion of money being wired about so cavalierly. We spent the morning discovering that the peach was as extinct in North America as the dinosaur. We began to doubt that we had ever eaten one – yet in the past we had seen pictures of little girls communing with them and we knew that the word, however mythical, had passed into the English language. Abandoning the search, we stopped in front of a news stand and assuaged our boredom by buying picture postcards of all Washington's churches and sending them with pious messages to our irreligious friends.

Four o'clock rolled along Pennsylvania avenue and greeted us at the door of the Romanoff garage; in half an hour we had

added one more rattle to the ancient bridge over which the fugitives from Bull Run had streamed on an afternoon of panic and terror, and our four wheels rolled onto the soil of the Old Dominion.

A cool wind blew, faint and fresh. Slow short hills climbed in green tranquility toward a childish sky. And already there were ante-bellum landscapes – featuring crazy cabins inhabited by blue-black gentlemen and their ladies in red-checked calico. The south now – its breath was warm upon us. The trees no longer exfloreated in wild haste, as though they feared that October was already scurrying over the calendar – their branches gestured with the faintly tired hauteur of a fine lady's hand. The sun was at home here, touching with affection the shattered ruins of once lovely things. Still, after fifty years we could see the chimneys and wall corners that marked the site of old mansions – which we peopled with pleasant ghosts. Here under the gay wisteria life at its mellowest had once flourished – not as on Long Island with streets and haste and poverty and pain just twenty miles away, but in a limitless empire whose radius was the distance a good horse could travel in a morning and whose law was moulded only of courtesy and prejudice and flame.

And at the moment when we became aware of Virginia's picturesqueness we became aware also of its selfconscious insistence on this picturesqueness. It seemed to cherish its anachronisms and survivals, its legend of heroism in defeat and of impotence before the vulgarities of industrialism, with too shrill an emphasis. For all its gorgeous history there was something tinny and blatant in its soul.

We reached Fredericksburg about five. I tried to reconstruct the battle from memory – I was not there but I had read about it – and failed wretchedly. I located the river, the hill and the town, but they had become changed around in some curious manner since the Civil War and they no longer worked. A garrulous gasoline dispenser told us that his father had participated in the battle and gave us his idea of the position of the contending troops. But if he was correct the history books have all erred grievously, three dozen generals have perjured themselves and Robert E. Lee was defending Washington.

At sunset we plunged into the Wilderness – the Wilderness where slain boys from Illinois and Tennessee and the cities of the gulf still slept in the marshes and the wooded swamps – but over the bloody ground there was only the drone of the cicadas now and the sway of the lush vines. The road began' to wind between stagnant pools and crepuscular marshes and each time we emerged for a moment into view of the open sky we found it a darker blue and saw that the mouth of the next tunnel of grey gloom was denser and less opaque. Finally we came out of a green subway to find that it was half-past seven and full night. An uncanny nervousness began to come over me and when the next copse approached I treaded the road with breathless care – sensitive to a certain profanity when the deep hum of our great motor burst against the ominous leafy walls.

And it was at this point, with danger, had I known it, just around the corner, that Zelda decided that she wanted to drive. We stopped in the first clearing and I yielded up the wheel.

Ten minutes passed. It was necessary to drive slowly, and, as well as I could determine from Dr Jones's Guide Book, which I fingered unsatisfactorily by the light of a recent acquisition, an electric torch, we were still forty-two miles from Richmond – still well over an hour away. My uncanny predilection now resolved itself into the specific dread that Lazarus would give up the ghost with a nerve-shaking roar in the middle of a wooded swamp, and that I should have to remove him at the mercy of bullfrogs and banshees and the dead of battles long ago.

With a sort of aching hollowness I saw the next woods approach. The leaves splashed away before us and Zelda followed a needing emptiness, confused by the cock-eyed slant of the headlights, of which one sought the road beneath and the other, with appalling perversity, illuminated the roof of the arboreal world.

We drifted down a sudden incline and, still descending slowly, were rounding the surface of a dark pool, when a man stepped suddenly into the road about twenty yards in front of us. The glare of the depressed headlight fell on him for a moment and we saw that his face, brown or white, we could not determine which, was covered with a black mask, and that in his right hand was the glint of a revolver. The impression he made, vivid and startling, endured for a moment; I remember that he uttered an indistinguishable shout and that I yelled 'Look out!' to Zelda, and tried to slide us both down low in the seat – then, all in the same minute, there was a swift rush of cool air, there was a black-banded face not ten yards away – and I realized with a sort of awed exhilaration that Zelda had stepped on the accelerator. With a gasping cry the masked man took a quick sidestep and avoided the bull-like leap of the car by inches – then we were by and away, rocking blindly, skidding around turns – hunched down in our seats to avoid a shot, until we could scarcely see the way.

We rounded half a dozen bends still traveling at over forty miles an hour before I found breath to gasp: 'You stepped on it!'

'Yes,' sighed Zelda laconically.

'That was the thing to do but – I'd have slowed up I think – involuntarily.'

'I didn't mean to step on it,' she confessed surprisingly. 'I was trying to stop and I got mixed up and stepped on the wrong thing.'

We laughed and began to chatter feverishly as our taut nerves relaxed. But it was pitch dark, with Richmond far off, and when I discovered that there was but a single gallon of gasoline in the tank I felt again that uncanny hollowness. The shadowy phantoms of an hour before had given way to images of murderous negroes hiding in bottomless swamps and of waylaid travelers floating on their faces in black pools. I regretted violently that I had not bought a revolver in Washington.

Under the torch I looked at the guide-book map. There seemed to be but one settlement between us and Richmond, a small dot which bore the sinister name of Niggerfoot. Ah – let it lack churches and schools and chambers of commerce, but let it not lack gasoline!

Ten minutes later it came into view as a single light which divided itself presently into the half a dozen yellow windows of a country store. As we came closer we could distinguish the blurred sounds of many voices within. The weird mood into which our later experience had projected us made us loathe to stop – but we had no choice. I drew up alongside, where we were immediately joined by two aged negroes and a quartet of little black boys from whom I demanded gasoline. After the manner of their race they tried to avoid the issue – the gasoline was locked up for the night; it was impossible to get at it.

They shook their heads. They mumbled melancholy and ineffectual protests. As I grew more vehement, their stubborn stupidity grew hazy rather than gave way – one of the old men vanished into the darkness to return with a yellow buck of reasonable age. Then there was more arguing until finally one of the little boys went sullenly in search of a pail. When he returned a second boy carried the pail up the road, and fifteen minutes later an absolutely new boy arrived with three quarts of gasoline.

Meanwhile I had gone into the store for cigarettes and found myself enclosed immediately in a miasmatic atmosphere which left on me a vivid and unforgettable impression. I could not say clearly even now what was going on inside that store – a moonshine orgy, a pay-day gambling bout, something more sinister than these or perhaps not sinister at all. Nor could I determine whether the man who waited on me was black or white. But this I know – that the room was simply jammed with negroes and that the moral and physical aura which they cast off was to me oppressive and obscene. I was glad to find my way outside again into the hot dark where the moon had risen and the gasoline carrier had come into sight and the two old negro men were exclaiming aloud in falsetto cackles at the size and thunder of the Expenso engine.

About nine o'clock the road became hard and smooth beneath us and trembling lights glimmered into our consciousness until the city, around which four bloody years had centered, developed on all sides of us.

But entry into Richmond was, we discovered, a difficult matter. The city was set behind impregnable barriers. The streets we tried were in various conditions of cavernous repair and adorned with romantic red lanterns – a sort of mole's carnival. I began to think that the defenses erected for the crisis of 1865 had never been removed and were still defiantly repelling the Yankee invader – but they yielded to us at last and permitted us to arrive at our inevitable destination, the Best Hotel in Town...

'Good evening,' I said hastily to the clerk. 'We're touring through from Connecticut and we want a room with a bath.' I smiled ingratiatingly. 'We've got to have a bath with a room.'

It was essentially the same speech that had gained us entrance to the New Willard. It served the same purpose here; it did more than that, for they gave us the bridal suite – an immense and imponderable affair as melancholy as a manufacturer's tomb. With the water steaming into the tub we discussed the day. We had left only one state – or district – behind us, but we had traversed a hundred and thirty-three miles and tasted drama. All afternoon impression after impression had taken us by storm leading up to the climax of the lone highwayman in the swamp. But one more happening was destined to disturb further the shattered equanimity of the day. It was not another highwayman. It was a piece of tongue.

It lay quietly and comparatively unobtrusively in the center of the carpet and after delicately stirring with the tip of a pencil I saw that it had been lying there several weeks.

Then I turned quickly away from it as I heard Zelda's voice speaking tensely, passionately, over the telephone–

'Hello! This is room two-ninety-one! What do you *mean* by renting us a room with *meat* all over the floor?'

A pause. The whole telephone system of the hotel seemed to me to be vibrating with fury–

'Yes, "meat all over the floor"! Old dead *meat!* I think it's perfectly *terrible!* ... All right! *Right* away!'

She banged up the phone and turned on me an outraged countenance.

'How *utt*erly disgusting!'

Five minutes later, after Zelda was enveloped in the steam of her hot bath, there was a knock at the door.

I opened it upon a harassed, apologetic clerk. Behind him stood three colored assistants bearing large shovels.

'Pardon me,' he said deferentially. 'The lady called up to complain that the floor was covered with dead meat.'

I pointed sternly. 'Look!' I said.

He stared with polite eyes.

'Where?'

The tongue, being still of a reddish hue, was almost imperceptible against the lugubrious crimson carpet. At length he made it out and motioned a negro forward to secure it.

'Now, where's the rest, sir?'

'I'm sure I don't know,' I answered stiffly. 'You'll have to locate it yourself.'

After a puzzled search behind the radiators, in the clothes closet and under the bed, the negroes reported that there was no more tongue. Shouldering their great shovels, they moved toward the door.

'Is there anything else?' asked the night clerk, anxiously. 'I'm very sorry about this, sir. There's never been any old meat in any of the bedrooms before tonight, sir.'

'I hope not,' I said firmly. 'Good night.'

He closed the door.

## VI

And now a day of depression – inaugurated by the garage man of Richmond. He was concise and specific in his information. The body of the Rolling Junk was split almost in two, and was about to fall off the car. It must be welded on in a blacksmith's shop.

We wandered about Richmond, drenched by an unbelievable heat and humidity. We visited the Confederate museum and pored for an hour over shredded battleflags and romantic sabres and grey uniform coats, and, as we passed from room to room, the proud splendor of each state's display was dimmed only a little by the interminable lists of living women who had managed in some way to get their names linked up with these trophies. The trophies needed no sponsoring by the Miss Rachael Marys and the Mrs Gladys Phoebes whom one pictured as large-bosomed and somewhat tiresome old ladies engaged in voluble chatter upon their ancestors in the sitting rooms and boarding houses of Macon, Georgia.

This exhausted Richmond – we discovered nothing else of any possible interest. After noon the humidity became oppressive sultriness, and the scattered curlicues of clouds began to solve a great jigsaw puzzle in the sky. We went to the black-smith and found that he had only just begun his soldering – because the garage man had discovered that the blotter had again escaped the tappets. We sat and stewed on the blacksmith's block.

We had planned to reach Oxford, North Carolina, before night, and Oxford was over a hundred and fifty miles away. When, as we were finally rolling out of the blacksmith's, Santa Claus blew into rubber butterflies, we began to despair.

When we moved out into the sultry countryside at last the sun was in shadow and the picture before us was as dispiriting as the view out of a dentist's window. The fields were green without freshness and the villages, where lanky men and boys gathered at the gasoline tanks to stare at our motor moved us to neither pastoral nor historical enthusiasm. We were not happy. The tyranny of tires weighed upon our spirits. There were so many weak spokes in one wheel that it was unsafe to run on it at over ten miles an hour. We used it merely for a spare wheel; upon it we limped slowly to the next garage after each catastrophe.

We talked now neither of biscuits nor of peaches. Having discussed them for one hundred and fifty hours with gradually diminishing energy, Zelda's imaginative appetite was at length satiated. And, on my part, I believe the sight of a peach or a biscuit would have gagged me. So Zelda sat all afternoon with Dr Jones' Guide Book in her hands, turning to the wrong page, giving erroneous directions and losing the place at crucial moments.

Just after six the dark came down in earnest. There was a mutter of thunder and out of the West came one of those fierce warm dusty winds which arouse uncanny discomfort with their high, bleak moanings and the touch of their hot, humid hands. The dark hindered our progress and we began to doubt that we could make North Carolina that night. It was still seventy miles away.

The wind was soon swollen into a dark gale and over the field toward us came the ponderous thresh of the rain. The sky was branded with a chain of flaming Zs and the thunder bowled sultry doom along the flat land. Then the rain sirened closer, washed over us, bringing with it the stinging deposits of the dust-laden wind. When the sand left our eyes Zelda hurriedly thumbed the guidebook and found a town named Clarksville about twelve miles ahead.

The name of the town was printed in large capitals and though its population was only five thousand we presupposed at least one tolerable hotel. The fact that it lay in Virginia was, of course, a moral loss – it would be the first time we had passed two nights in a single state.

I drove as fast as I dared into the blown darkness, but the way seemed interminable in the Byronic storm. We were relieved when, at last, Clarksville rolled up the road toward us. I left

Zelda to register at the Dominion Hotel, and went to find a garage. For once, perhaps because we had only gone one hundred and twelve miles, I had no list of suspicions and instructions to write out and hand to a sleepy-eyed attendant.

Returning I found that we were not nearly so well housed as the Rolling Junk. No food was obtainable in the hotel, so I went into a country store and bought two unappetizing egg-sandwiches from the unappetizing proprietor. These I took up to Zelda who, with great presence of mind, threw them immediately out of the window.

Our room was bare and it had a bath with it. Into the bath ran ice cold water. Zelda swam in it as a matter of principle, and then – chiefly out of spite – taunted me into a feeble imitation. It was a miserable, shivering, depressed pretense of a bath, but when it was over I made the usual virtue of it and strutted around the room like a dollar-a-year man after his daily dozen.


## VII


Sunday morning, Zelda awoke and dressed herself in a white knickerbocker suit. Famished, we went downstairs and were served with an abominable breakfast that I nibbled at humbly but by which Zelda felt herself deliberately insulted. When we were leaving the hotel two fat ladies who were occupying the front steps stared at Zelda's knickerbockers and chattered violently to each other – whereupon Zelda, now in a raging mood, returned their stare and remarked in a perfectly audible, voice 'Look at those two *horrible* women!' I am aware that this phrase is of the type usually attributed to villainesses in sloppy fiction – showing that damp cornflakes have much the same effect as a stony heart.

Sunday in Virginia is a day of rest – gasoline is almost as hard to get as cigarettes, and we were glad when the North Carolina boundary grew near. Dr Janes's Guide Book had now resorted to sheer fiction – and cheap, trashy, sentimental fiction at that.

While I favor discreetly draping many of the facts of life, I call it a pernicious optimism that tries to pass off the rocky bed of a dried-out stream as a 'boulevard'. And the map was ornamented with towns, pops, corner stores and good roads that could have existed only in Dr Jones's rosy imagination.

About the time we crossed the white chalk line which divides Virginia from North Carolina, we became aware that some sort of dispute was taking place in the interior of the car. It began as a series of sullen mutters but soon the participants were involved in a noisy and metallic altercation. I gathered that things were being thrown... Dismounting, I crawled underneath and glared at the bottom of the car. It looked to me as it had always looked. There were some dark, mysterious rods and some dark iron pans and a great quantity of exhaust. We thought that perhaps we were out of gasoline and had the tank filled at the next station, but the pounding continued. We tried oil and water – even had the hood chamied off, but with no result. When we reached a town of the same size we sought out the largest garage and demanded an inspection.

After three men in overalls – Sunday was not a day of rest in North Carolina – had played around for a while on little wooden sidewalks that slid underneath the car, they all stood up in line and shook their heads in sad unison like a musical comedy chorus. Then they wheeled about and went away.

At this point there was a great roaring at the door, and in rode a tall young man driving a large and powerful Expenso, of the same type as ours. Without exactly looking at the young man, I began to mope disconsolately around my own car, shaking the wheels sternly and picking bits of dust off the fender – in short, giving the impression that I was only waiting for something or somebody before beginning to perform some significant mechanical action. The young man, having parked his Expenso, strolled over to look at mine.

'Trouble?' he demanded.

'Nothing much,' I answered grimly. 'It's all broken inside, that's all.'

'Your wheel's coming off,' he remarked dispassionately.

Oh, it's done that,' I assured him. 'It did that in Washington.'

'It's coming off again – from the inside.'

I smiled politely as though I had noticed it some time before. I took the wrench from the rear of the car and began to tighten the wheel.

'It's coming off from the *inside*. No use tightening it there – you'll have to take it off.'

I was somewhat confused, as I had not been previously aware that a wheel could come off from the inside as well as just come off, but I snapped my fingers and remarked:

'Of course. How stupid of me!'

When I had removed the wheel and leaned it up against the wall of the garage, I approached the axle under the now suspicious eye of the Expenso owner. Stare as I might, it looked to me exactly like any other axle, and I failed to perceive in it any qualities which would permit the wheel to come off from the inside. I tapped it tentatively. Then, from force of habit, I shook it. These two gestures having been observed in silence by the tall young man, I turned to him mildly.

'You're right,' I said. 'It was coming off from the inside.' Then I picked up the wheel and was about to replace it on the axle, when the Expenso owner gave a warning grunt, finished lighting a cigarette, and inquired solemnly:

'What you doing?'

'I'm putting it back.'

'What did you take it off for?'

He had me there. I had taken it off solely because he had told me to, yet somehow this didn't seem the right answer to his question.

'Because – why, to see if it was coming off from the inside.'

'Well, you saw, didn't you?'

This was unfair. It was not playing the game. I decided to defy him, decided not to.

'Why – no,' I muttered weakly. 'It looked all right to me.'

The suspicion in his eye changed to certainty. He glanced in at the knickerbocker-clad Zelda, seated in nonchalant gravity in the front seat. Then he looked at me.

'Where are your tools?' he said briefly. 'Get your other wrench.'

'I haven't any tools.'

I had thrown aside all pretense. I stood before him naked in my mechanical ignorance. But my avowal, made in sheer helplessness, had its effect. He dropped his cigarette and stared at me open-mouthed. He had a tremendous mouth.

'No *tools*!'

'I have no tools,' I repeated meekly.

I had shocked him. I had stuck a sharp iron into the heart of his morality. I had offended horribly against his spotless creed of the Expenso. In one minute I had passed from a place among the privileged into an outer, darker circle. I owned an Expenso? – then so much the more blasphemous if I was not worthy of my property.

He called brusquely to a garage helper. 'Here! Let's have a C wrench.'

Iron in a novel shape appeared, and I thought how wonderful is civilization. Actuated by a natural baseness, I shrank back from the car as though fearing the coolness of the metal. But he tossed the article at me relentlessly, and I took it, approached the axle, adjusted the wrench feebly and began to turn whatever there was to turn.

The Expenso expert stood over me sternly. 'No,' he said indignantly. *'Tighten* it.'

Had he ordered me to eat it I should have been no more helpless. I dropped the wrench to my side and stared at him with what I suspected was a silly expression. Zelda's face was hidden sleepily in her hands. She had abandoned me, without so much as a wink, to this man's devices. Even the garage force had moved off and away, lest they be called upon.

'Here!' Cato strode toward me. With a mixture of shame and relief I yielded up the wrench to him. He reached for one of the sliding floors, dropped knee upon it and, without difficulty, adjusted the wrench. I crowded up upon him, obscenely interested. Then my hopes were dashed to the ground. With a straightforward movement of his shoulders that seemed somehow to express the emotion of utter contempt which just failed to show in his face, he stood up and pointed to the wrench. 'That's the way,' he said. He meant, 'Get to work! You dog, you! How dare you own an Expenso!' But he said aloud: 'Get some oil from over there in the corner and use it before you begin.'

Then, as I moved away to get the oil, he got in his horrible, insidious touch – something so subtle that it could have sprung only from a lack of subtlety, something so utterly devastating that when Zelda told me of it later, half an hour later – my brain reeled and the world became black as death. For the man moved upon Zelda, commanded her politeness by using the advantage he held over me, and after a few misleading preliminaries said:

'It's a pity that a nice girl like you should be let to wear those clothes.'

He was looking at her knickerbockers. It was fifty years of provincialism speaking; it was the negative morality of the poor white – and yet it filled me with helpless and inarticulate rage. But Zelda's coolness in the face of such a charge must have flabbergasted him. He had trusted too much in his moral advantage over me, for he did not annoy her farther. If he had, I do not doubt that he would have met with the same fate as the two old women in Clarksville.

We got ourselves eventually from the garage. The wheel was no longer coming off 'from the inside'; the noise had ceased; all was serene. We confided ourselves to Dr Jones and started south through North Carolina. We attained Durham, but, due to the fact that the rain had begun to fall, we omitted to celebrate the fact that we had now gone six hundred miles and were half way to Montgomery. We ate a luscious watermelon, which cheered us a little – but we could not erase it from our minds that, so long as Zelda wore her white knickerbockers, the surrounding yokelry regarded us with cold, priggish superiority, as 'sports'. We were in Carolina and we had not conducted ourselves sartorially as the Carolinians.

After Durham the sun came out and shone heavily down upon the worst roads in the world. But they were the best roads, we were assured both by Dr Jones and by a high yellow nigger with green eyes, between Durham and Greensboro. In that case the other roads must have been planted with barbed-wire entanglements. If you can imagine an endless rocky gully, rising frequently in the form of unnavigable mounds to a slope of sixty degrees, a gully covered with from an inch to a foot of grey water mixed with solemn soggy clay of about the consistency of cold cream and the adhesiveness of triple glue; if you drove an ambulance over shelled roads in France and can conceive of all the imperfections of all those roads placed within forty miles – then you have a faint conception of the roads of upper North Carolina.

With a patient fortitude we jogged left and we jogged right and we jogged both directions together; we groaned laboriously up and slid perilously down. We traversed whole stretches that would not have been fit boulevards for baby tanks. After a while we began to meet other tourists – flivvers up to their hips in mud, immersed so deep that only the driver's eyes were visible; flivvers traveling in ruts that were deep as graves and wide as footpaths, and, most tragic of all, bubbles where flivvers had recently sunk out of sight with their intrepid crews, to be heard from no more.

'Any better along where you come from?' they would shout, unless their mouths were below the mud surface; and I would always answer, 'Worse!' But I was always wrong, for the further we went the worse it grew. For the first time I felt a sort of pride in the achievements of the Rolling Junk. Erratic it might be, but it had a broad shouldered sturdiness and an indomitable ruggedness when faced with a material obstacle. It could scale a precipice or ford a muddy stream impassible to a smaller, lighter car.

We had little else now about which to be enthusiastic. Biscuits and peaches had paled; the joy of 'surprising mother and father' had been talked to a slow death; our suitcases bulged both with laundry and with the mud of eight states and a district. And, lastly, we were running short of money.

To be exact, there remained twenty-five dollars and some brown and silver change. When I had written from Washington for money I had directed, with an unjustifiable optimism, that it be sent *not* to Greens*boro*, North Carolina – which we were now approaching – but to *Greenville*, South Carolina, which was two hundred miles farther south.

At twilight we came into Greensboro, which offered the O. Henry Hotel, an elaborate hostelry, at sight of which Zelda decided to slip on a skirt over her knickerbockers. This time I instructed the garage man *not* to inspect the Rolling Junk – nay, not even to look at it closely. If there was anything the matter with it we couldn't afford to have it fixed anyhow. It was better not to know. Then we bathed in faintly reddish water which lent a pleasant crimson glow to the bath-tub, and ate a large dinner. This last, with the tip, used up four dollars and fifty cents of our money, but we were too tired to care.

# Part Three

Greenville or starve! The Rolling Junk eyed us with reproachful lamps as though it knew that it had been cheated of its customary physical examination. We explained to it that our garage and hotel bills, our gasoline and oil, our breakfast and the black man's tip had reduced our capital to six dollars and thirty cents.

The sunshine was sparkling, and it was only half past eight.

'I'm glad the roads are good,' said Zelda. 'We can do two hundred miles before sunset. We've never started this early before.'

Insidious roads! – brick now as though to make up for the recent gullies.

'Step on it!' urged Zelda.

'I was about to.'

Two hundred miles to money, two hundred miles to tires, repairs, shelter and food.

So I stepped on it. It was the first time I had tested the speed of the Rolling Junk – the Boston Post Road was monopolized by gigantic trucks which made racing precarious. But now – the smooth brick of the road stretched seductively before us, without another automobile, or a street car or a cross-street or a turning. And slowly the indicator on the dashboard mounted to forty, to fifty, then crept slowly to fifty-five, receded to fifty-three and, as if reconsidering, climbed rapidly up to sixty-one.

'Are you stepping on it?'

'Yes.'

'It's not so nice as an airplane,' she remarked cryptically.

I had been saving up for an ultimate burst of speed, but at this I pressed my foot down until the accelerator was touching the floor. With almost a leap the Rolling Junk increased its pace – we seemed to be flying – the speedometer shot up to

73

sixty-four, then, point by point, battled a hazardous course to seventy-four, where it tried to settle, reaching for seventy-five on slight downgrades and dropping to seventy-three on hills.

At that rate we would have arrived in Montgomery at half past four that day – it was unbelievable – of course we couldn't keep it up – we didn't expect to get to Montgomery until the day after tomorrow – still – the wind was roaring – the road was contracting before us like a rubber band – momentarily I expected one of the wheels to flash by us or else crush up on its spokes like an egg – Kingdom Come –

Ten, fifteen minutes passed. The road, barren of any traffic, stretched on indefinitely. We must have covered twenty miles with scarcely a change of pace. I was imagining a boulevard like this stretching between Westport and Montgomery. I was imagining that I had the fastest car ever made – it could travel three miles a minute. At that rate we could have left Westport after lunch and arrived at Montgomery in time for dinner–

After a while excessive motion began to weary me. I saw the suspicion of a turn about two miles ahead and taking my foot slowly from the accelerator reduced our speed to forty miles an hour – at which pace we seemed to be merely crawling. It was at this point that I became aware of a new sound – a persistent and obnoxious sound, distinct and differentiated from the sound of our motor. At the same moment Zelda glanced around.

'Lord!' she cried. 'It's a motorcycle policeman!'

I tried to come down as unostentatiously as possible to a modest thirty. But my efforts at camouflage were feeble – as transparent as the start of innocent surprise I gave when the policeman rode up alongside and greeted me with a prolonged grunt. At his bidding I came to a full stop.

'Well!' he said with a ferocious countenance.

'Well?' I answered brilliantly. I felt that I should have offered him a drink or at least a piece of candy or something – but I could offer him nothing.

'Going seventy miles an hour, weren't you?'

Instead of correcting him, I merely lifted my eyebrows in horror and exclaimed reproachfully, as though I could hardly believe my ears.

'Seventy miles an *hour!*'

'Seventy miles an *hour!*' he mimicked. 'Turn around and folla me back to the codehouse.'

'Officer,' I said briskly, 'we're in a hurry. We–'

'I saw you were in a hurry. I can tell from my own speedometeh how fast you were goin'.'

'We're in a – in a *terrible hurry!*' I insisted, thinking wildly of the six dollars and thirty cents in my pocket. Suppose the fine were ten dollars! Would we have to languish in jail? A shiver passed over me. 'Isn't there anything we can do?'

'Well,' he said glibly, 'the fine for first offense speeding is five dollahs. If you don't want to come back to the codehouse you can give me the five dollahs and I'll see it gets to the jedge.'

I had my suspicions that this transaction was unofficial – that the judge would never 'hear tell' of my money. But I did believe that the fine would reach that figure, perhaps more, and the return to the 'codehouse' would be an expense of both time and gasoline. So I handed over a precious bill whereat the guardian of the roads, thanked me, tipped his hat and drove hastily away.

'Now how much money have we?' asked Zelda crossly.

'Dollar thirty.'

'If you hadn't slowed down he couldn't have caught us.'

'We'd have had to slow down eventually. And he'd have telephoned ahead or else shot at our tires.'

'He couldn't have hurt them much.'

We sat in stony silence between the five dollar bill and Charlotte.

In Charlotte we lunched. We lunched on the thirty cents, reserving the dollar for an emergency. Zelda had an ice cream cone, and a hot dog and a nut bar. I digested a fifteen cent dish which was resting on a lunch-counter, under the transparent alias of meat and potatoes. Feeling much worse we drove out of Charlotte and took the road to Greenville – or rather did not take the road to Greenville. Due to a growing vagueness on the part of Dr Jones we started back toward New York and rode in fatuous ignorance for twelve miles. By that time it had become utterly impossible to force the road and the guide book into any sort of agreement, even though we let trees pass as telegraph poles and counted mileposts as schoolhouses. We grew nervous. We spoke to a farmer. He laughed and said he'd have to tell his wife about this.

It was all very discouraging. We passed back through Charlotte – it looked even less attractive to us than it had before. But hardly were we well in the country again when we noticed that the apparently smooth road on which we were driving had grown unaccountably rough. I dismounted suspiciously – sure enough, Hercules had given up the ghost.

I put on the spare wheel with its new tire, but no sooner had it touched the ground than one of its spokes gave way. The situation was frightful – we had one good wheel and one good tire, but they were not together. Ah, if the wheel would only keep its shape until we reached a garage, if the garage man would only make the necessary change for one dollar!

Crawling along at ten miles an hour – at which rate we would have reached Montgomery in six days – we came to a country garage at three o'clock. We were very unhappy. I told the proprietor what I wanted and when I had finished he named his price. It was – here we held our breaths – one dollar.

Greenville was still one hundred miles farther south. One drop too little of gasoline, one more puncture, and we were done.

And then five miles from the South Carolina border, we obtained a succulent revenge for the humiliation heaped upon us by the scornful and highly moral Expenso owner the day before. It was necessary that this revenge take place in North

Carolina – had it occurred ten miles further south and in the sister state I would have borne the scar of the earlier encounter forever. As it is, I bear no malice.

The incident began as inauspiciously as the catastrophe of the day before. In fact, the Rolling Junk became noisily temperamental and I was compelled to stop.

'What is it?' Zelda's voice was tense with alarm. 'Is the wheel coming off from the inside again?'

'I think it's the motor.'

'Is it coming off?'

'I don't know. I think it's going out.'

As a matter of form I raised the hood and gazed at the mass of iron and tin and grease within. Probably if I had been a giant thirty-three yards tall, with a hand three yards long, who could have taken up the Rolling Junk and given it a *real* shake, it would have started, very much on the principle of a refractory watch.

We waited fifteen minutes. A farmer rolled stiffly down the road in a flivver. I waved at him wildly, but he took me for a hold-up man and seemed not a little startled as he went by.

We waited another fifteen minutes. Another car came into sight far down the road.

'Look, Zelda–' I began – ceased, for she was in a state of unusual activity. Like lightning she produced a disk-shaped box and became absorbed in the passionate pigmentation of her face – her hands ran like serpents through her bobbed hair, giving its permanent wave a jaunty blouse.

'You go way,' she said shortly.

'Go way?'

'Turn in that gate there and sit behind the wall.'

'Why the–'

'Hurry up! Before that car comes over the next hill.'

I had begun to get a glimmer of her idea. Obediently I ran back to the designated gate and concealed myself behind the very obligingly convenient wall.

The car dropped over the hill, grew larger, passed me with a whiff of oily dust. I saw it flash by the Rolling Junk and then, about twenty yards farther on, come to a precipitous stop. It backed with a scampish eagerness until it was beside the Expenso. Though I could see neither its driver nor Zelda, I gathered that they were in conversation. Then, after a moment, a figure dismounted from the other car and raised one side of the Rolling Junk's hood. He peered at the engine, nodded boastfully, comprehensively, smiled superiorly at Zelda and returned to his own car for tools. A minute later he was lying on his back underneath our car and I heard a clanking that delighted my heart.

Five minutes passed. He emerged several times to wipe the white July dew from his brow and to converse with Zelda. When he emerged the last time he buttoned up the hood. Zelda, evidently acting according to his direction, started the motor – it gave out a healthy, robust sound. The Samaritan replaced the tools in his car and, returning, set one foot on the running board of the Rolling Junk and began an animated conversation. I judged that it was time for my re-appearance – I walked out into the road and toward them, mildly whistling 'The Beal Street Blues.'

They both turned. The man's eyes, the eyes possibly of a country banker's son, looked upon me in dismay – they were eyes, I am glad to say, very much like those of the Expenso owner of the day before.

'Oh you're back!' exclaimed Zelda pleasantly. 'Did you find a phone? It doesn't matter if you didn't because this gentleman was kind enough to fix what was wrong.'

'That was mighty nice of him,' I said brazenly.

The man gazed from one to the other of us with a strained stare. Then from sheer embarrassment he made the remark that put him utterly in my power.

'Oh,' he ejaculated, involuntarily and in an obviously disappointed voice, 'I thought you were alone.'

'No,' said Zelda gravely, 'my husband's with me,' and she added cruelly, 'I never tour alone.'

I climbed in beside her and took the wheel.

'It certainly was awfully kind of you, and I'm very much obliged.'

The banker's son grunted, stood there staring at me wordlessly, with pendant brows. I threw the car into first.

'We've got to hurry on,' I suggested.

Zelda thanked him profusely. We slid off. When we had gone fifty yards I looked back and discovered that he had turned his car completely around and started off in the direction from which he had come.

Considerably cheered we drove on, heading into a pale yellow sun which hovered over the black and green highlands in the distance.

'Gosh!' exclaimed Zelda in sudden dismay. She was staring blankly at an open page of Dr. Jones' guide book.

'What's the matter?'

'There's a toll bridge between North and South Carolina, and we haven't a nickel!'

Almost at the same moment it came into view. For the second time that day I stepped hard on the accelerator. We flew down a short hill, thundered on to the rattling bridge and raced madly across to the friendly shore. Zelda glancing back, reported that a funny little man had come out of a funny little house and was waving his arms passionately. But we were safe in South Carolina.

Safe? – At seven o'clock we smelled the rusty metallic sweat of the engine. The oil register showed zero. We became very sad. We tried to fool the engine by running very fast – so we groaned up a hill and down into a city named for the stoical Lacedemonians – Spartansburg. The game was up – we had no money to buy oil and we could go no farther.

'It's my birthday,' said Zelda, suddenly. This somehow astonished me more than anything that had happened that day.

'I just remembered.'

She had just remembered!

'Let us go to the police station and give ourselves up,' she said. In conventional predicaments she is without resources.

'No,' said I. 'We will go to the Spartansburg telegraph office and persuade them to wire ahead to Greenville for our money.'

Zelda doubted whether the Spartansburg agent would trust us. Also, being from Alabama, and having therefore no confidence in Progress, she did not believe that the money was in Greenville anyhow.

We reached the telegraph office and, peering in through the windows after the immemorial manner of the poor, we saw that the station agent was a young male of kindly countenance. We entered. He consented to wire for us. We sat outside in the

Rolling Junk for half an hour, enviously watching well-fed people pass, and then the operator came out and told us that we were no longer penniless, but possessed of three hundred dollars. We almost wept upon him, but he refused a gratuity.

We left the Rolling Junk to be thoroughly doctored, and dined in a Greek restaurant, where we were served by a handsome Spartan with a cake to celebrate Zelda's birthday. To conclude fittingly a day on which we had been guilty of speeding, bribery, toll-dodging and obtaining help under false pretenses, we purchased many curious postcards adorned with plush and frosting and moral messages, and sent them broadcast through the land. That day we had gone one hundred and eighty miles, and the backbone of the trip was broken at last.

## IX

Next day the triumphant Rolling Junk, bulging with oil, plunged through impassable streams and surmounted monstrous crags. A garage man in Anderson told us that the Expenso had one hundred different ailments and would not last out another hundred miles, but they were all new ailments, so we laughed in his face. We were going to arrive in Montgomery in time for dinner the following evening. We even considered wiring ahead lest Zelda's parents be dangerously shocked when we appeared, but we decided against it, for we had kept our secret too long to relinquish it now.

The collapse of Sampson near the Georgia line was only a comic calamity, for was not old Lazarus clinging firmly to the left rear wheel, the last survivor of the five tires with which we had left Westport? – brave Lazarus with his bald spots and his abrasions. Santa Claus, Hercules, Sampson, as well as the tire we had abandoned to make chewing gum for Mr. Bibelick in Philadelphia, were all departed to the rubber heaven where nails and glass exist not and one is always a spare.

We crossed into Georgia by a long iron bridge and burst into a long yell of jubilation, for Georgia was next to Alabama and Zelda had often motored from Montgomery to football games in Columbus or Atlanta. The sandy roads took on a heavenly color, the glint of the trees in the sun was friendly, the singing negroes in the field were the negroes of home. In every town through which we passed, Zelda would declare enthusiastically that she knew dozens of boys who lived there if she could only just remember their names. Several times she went to the extent of entering drug stores and futilely thumbing directories in search of gallants who had once danced in the dawn at Sewanee or Tech or the University of Alabama, but the months had washed away all except a dozen fragmentary first names and a few shadowy memories.

We drew near Athens, the seat of the University of Georgia. Had we broken down irretrievably at this point I believe we would have had ourselves towed into Montgomery by horses rather than arrive without the Rolling Junk. We were only two hundred and fifty miles away, and we decided to sleep in Athens, rise before dawn and cover all the remaining distance on the morrow. We had never done two hundred and fifty miles in a day – but the roads down here were smooth and dry and we knew that we could make better time than in the Carolinas.

In the hotel we were given a salesman's display room – a huge chamber with sample tables and a business-like air, haunted by the pleasant ghosts of lazy southern commerce. In the streets, the dark balmy streets, we watched strolling girls in their stiff muslin dresses, girls with too much rouge, but cool and soft-voiced and somehow charming here under the warm southern moon. Our evening round of postcards seemed almost out of place – we were living again the life and moving in the atmosphere we had known so well in Montgomery two years before. I saw some numbers of Old King Brady and Young Wild West on a news stand, and fascinated by their colored covers I bought half a dozen. We read them in bed until nine o'clock when, in accordance with our plans for the next day, we turned out the light.

The telephone tolled violently at four, and we awoke with all the excitement of early Christmas morning. We dressed in a sleepy haze and stumbled down to breakfast – but there was no breakfast! A drowsy night-clerk stared at us in scorn as we dragged our bags through the lobby. A drowsy watchman yawned and spluttered as I entered the garage across the street where burned a blue and solitary light. Then we were in the deep dusty leather seats whose feel we knew so well, tearing along through the last end of the darkness toward Atlanta.

Something more than half awake we watched the morning develop in hamlet after hamlet as we went by. In one place milk was being delivered, in the next a drowsy housewife was shaking something – perhaps a child – on the back porch. Then for an hour we passed group after group of negroes bound singing for the cotton fields and the work of the hot hours.

Just after eight there was Camp Gordon where once upon a time I had taught Wisconsin country boys the basic principles of 'squads right' through two chilly months; and, later, smiling Peach Tree Street beamed upon us with a hundred mansions of opulent Atlanta set among bright groves of pine and palm.

We stopped at a little cafe for breakfast – then out on the road again and racing a flivver along the hard dust in a delirium of delight. Why not? When evening came we would have travelled twelve hundred miles, traversed the entire coast of a great nation and vindicated the Rolling Junk against all the garage-men in Christendom. Why, we were so proud now that when a drawling gasoline-jerker gaped at our Connecticut license we told him that Connecticut was five thousand miles away and that we had driven it in three days.

It was not only of ourselves that we boasted to each other, but of the Rolling Junk.

'Remember how she took those Carolina Hills?'

'And went through those muddy streams where the other cars had stopped?'

'And ate up that stretch of road near Charlotte?'

'Oh, it's a wonderful car, I think. It has its faults, of course, but it certainly has power.'

'Good old Expenso!'

At noon we came to West Point, which, contrary to general report, is not a military academy, but only the town that separates Georgia from Alabama. Over the bridge and onto the soil of Zelda's native state, the cradle of the Confederacy, the utter heart of the old south, the ground of our dreams and destination. But we were too maudlin with excitement now to experience a distinct territorial thrill and set it off from other and equally importunate emotions.

The afternoon began in heat. The road ran through sandy swamps full of damp evaporation and under heavy growth of Spanish moss where the atmosphere was like a conservatory. We stopped at Opelika for gasoline. Just next door was Auburn, seat of the Alabama Polytechnic Institute. Here Zelda had known the greatest gaiety of her youth, for Auburn belonged primarily to Montgomery as its sister college, the University, belonged to Birmingham. Auburn – in many hurried letters had she aroused my uneasiness with the news that she was just starting up to Auburn to attend a dance, watch a football game, or merely spend an idle day!

Through Tuskegee then as the heat of the afternoon was drifting off from the land like smoke. We left something behind us in Tuskegee. We did not know it at the time and it was better that we should not know. Into a tranquil street of the reposeful city we had dropped an intrinsic part of the Rolling Junk – from Tuskegee onward we were without the services of a battery. It had jumped with a neat and imperceptible movement from the car. Had we stopped now and shut off the motor, if only for a minute, no power we could have wielded would have started us again.

We spoke little now. When automobiles passed we craned our necks looking for familiar faces. Suddenly Zelda was crying, crying because things were the same and yet were not the same. It was for her faithlessness that she wept and for the faithlessness of time. Then into the ever-changing picture swam the little city crouching under its trees for shelter from the heat.

Simultaneously one of the most ludicrous signs that I have ever seen caught my eye. It was an enormous faded, battered affair which hung by one ear from a post set awry by the road-side. In almost illegible letters, erratically dotted with defunct electric bulbs, it proclaimed that this was:

MONTGOMERY
'Your Opportunity'

We were in Montgomery – it was breathless, unbelievable. A journey by train is somehow convincing. Sleep bridges the mysterious gap. You feel that the intrinsic change from one locality to another has taken place in the night – but we found it impossible to believe, now, that one day's trip had been hitched securely on to another day's trip and had led us *here*. – Why, Montgomery was on another plane and we were actually rolling into it, right down Dexter Avenue as though it had been a street in Westport!

It was five o'clock. We were sure that Judge and Mrs Sayre would be on the porch. Our hearts thumped desperately – Twelve Hundred Miles! 'Oh, hello!' we would say – or would we be calm? Or would we faint dead away? Or would the Rolling Junk crumble to pieces before our eyes? Or what would express the tremendous vitality of our success – and the unexpected sadness of the journey's end, of the south itself, of the past we two had had together in this town.

We turned a last corner and craned our eyes to see. We stopped the car in front of Zelda's house.

There was no one on the porch. Fumbling at the door handle we descended from the car and ran up the front steps. My eye caught sight of half a dozen newspapers on the porch rolled into cylinders for quick delivery and a horrible presentiment swept over me. Zelda was at the closed door, her hand was on the knob.

'Why,' she cried, 'It's locked! Why, it's locked!'

I was thunderstruck.

'It's locked!' her voice was quite wild. 'They're not here!'

I tried the door. I counted the papers.

'They've been gone three days.'

'How terrible.' Her lip was trembling. I tried to think of a possible hope.

'They're probably at – out in the country or something. They'll probably be back tomorrow.' But the blinds were down. There was an air of desertion about it all.

'Why, my own house is locked!' Her tone was unbelieving – almost terrified.

Then a woman's voice from the lawn – Zelda turned and recognized her next door neighbor.

'Zelda Sayre, what are you doing down here?'

'My house is locked,' said Zelda tensely. 'What's the matter?'

'Why,' exclaimed the lady in a gentle surprise. 'Why, Judge and Mrs Sayre left Sunday night for Connecticut. I thought they were going to surprise you all. Why, Zelda, child, did you ride down here in an automobile?'

Zelda sat down suddenly on the steps and leaned her head against a post.

'That's what they said,' went on the lady in blue. 'They said they were going up to surprise you all.'

Ah, and it was bitter how well they had succeeded!

And so we came into port at last. I wonder if any such adventure is ever worth the enthusiasm put into it and the illusion lost. None but the very young or very old can afford such voluminous expectations and such bitter disappointment.

And if you had asked me then if I would do it again I would have answered with an emphatic No.

And yet – I have discovered in myself of late a tendency to buy great maps and pore over them, to inquire in garages as to the state of roads; sometimes, just before I go to sleep, distant Meccas come shining through my dreams and I tell Zelda of white boulevards running between green fields towards an enchanted sunset land. We have a good car – an *In*expenso and *not* a Rolling Junk – we look at it and wonder if it is sturdy and powerful enough to scale hills and plunge through streams like the other. We say now, when our opinion is asked, that there is no car like a good Expenso–

But the night grows late and I must round out the story. After the catastrophe we tried to start the car, to go to Zelda's sister, but we discovered that the battery was gone. Weeks later we learned, accidentally, that its mangled remains had been discovered in Tuskegee. The loss of the battery was the last blow and for a time the world seemed very dark. But the word blew around that Zelda was home and in a few minutes automobiles began to drive up to the door and familiar faces clustered around us – faces amused, astonished, sympathetic, but all animated by sincere pleasure in her return. So after a while our disappointment dimmed and faded away like all things.

We sold the Rolling Junk in Montgomery – we had decided, needless to say, to return to Westport by train. Of its subsequent history I know less than I would like to. It was passed on from a man I knew slightly to a man I did not know at all, and so I lost sight of it forever. Who knows? Perhaps it is still bowling along between Durham and Greensboro with faithful Lazarus resting on the rack at last. Perhaps less erratic and as robust as ever, it is still giving the lie to garage men and frightening highwaymen in Virginia swamps. Perhaps it is resolved into its component parts and has lost its identity and its mortal soul – or perished by fire or been drowned in the deep sea. My affection goes with you, Rolling Junk – with you and with all the faded trappings that have brightened my youth and glittered with hope or promise on the roads I have travelled – roads that stretch on still, less white, less glamorous, under the stars and the thunder and the recurrent inevitable sun.

# Notes

1. Reprinted in James Mellow, *Invented Lives* (Boston, 1984)
2. M.J. Bruccoli and Margaret M. Duggan (eds), *Correspondence of F. Scott Fitzgerald* (New York, 1980)
3. 'Scott Fitzgerald and the Jews', *Midstream*, 39, January 1993
4. Matthew J. Bruccoli (ed.), *As Ever, Scott Fitz: Letters between Fitzgerald and his literary agent Harold Ober 1919 to 1940* (London, 1973)
5. Footnote: In the *Fitzgerald Hemingway Annual* (1978)
6. Predictably, this did not start to appear until 1958, eighteen years after Fitzgerald's death.
7. 'They're a rotten crowd,' I shouted, across the lawn. 'You're worth the whole damn bunch put together.'

I've always been glad I said that. It was the only compliment I ever gave him, because I disapproved of him from beginning to end. First he nodded politely, and then his face broke into that radiant and understanding smile, as if we'd been in ecstatic cahoots on that fact all the time.

# Biographical note

Francis Scott Key Fitzgerald, better known as F Scott Fitzgerald, is widely regarded as one of the greatest American writers of the twentieth century.

Born in Minnesota in 1896, Fitzgerald was educated at various private schools in New York State and Minnesota, and at Princeton. Poor and unlikely to graduate, he dropped out and enlisted in the US Army. The First World War ended before Fitzgerald could be sent overseas, but it was while posted near Montgomery, Alabama, in 1918 that he met eighteen-year-old Zelda Sayre. A tumultuous courtship ensued, and they were eventually married in 1920 after the success of his first published novel, *This Side of Paradise*.

The Fitzgeralds embarked on a hedonistic, drink-fuelled celebrity lifestyle, further fuelled by the proceeds from Fitzgerald's second novel *The Beautiful and the Damned* (1922). Despite the commercial success of his writing, he was already experiencing money troubles as early as 1923, compounded by the failure of his first (and only) play, The Vegetable. This setback saw him depressed and drinking heavily.

In 1923 the Fitzgeralds moved to the French Riviera, where Scott finished writing his best-known novel, *The Great Gatsby*. Although it met with his most favourable critical reception to date, sales were relatively poor. During the 1920s Zelda's behaviour became increasingly erratic, and after she suffered her first mental breakdown in 1930 Scott was obliged to produce a steady output of magazine stories to pay for her treatment. She would be in and out of hospitals and institutions for the rest of her life.

It was not until 1934 that Fitzgerald was able to complete his fourth novel, *Tender is the Night*, which drew heavily on his experiences in Europe and of Zelda's illness. It was a critical and commercial failure, although it is now regarded as a classic novel of American marriage. His last years were spent in Hollywood, working as a scriptwriter to repay his debts and attempt to re-establish himself. Despite repeated attempts to stop drinking, he died suddenly in December 1940 at the age of forty-four. His fifth novel, *The Last Tycoon*, was published posthumously.

Zelda Fitzgerald died in a fire at a hospital in North Carolina in 1948.

Paul Theroux is an American novelist and travel writer. Born in Massachusetts, he has lived in Malawi, Uganda, Singapore and Britain, and now divides his time between Cape Cod and Hawaii. Since crossing Asia for *The Great Railway Bazaar* (1975), his journeys have included a circuitous tour of *China for Riding the Iron Rooster* (1988) and a journey from Cairo to Cape Town for *Dark Star Safari* (2002). His novels include *The Mosquito Coast* (1981), which won the James Tait Black Memorial Prize and was adapted for film. He is a fellow of the Royal Society of Literature and of the Royal Geographical Society.

Julian Evans grew up in Australia and London. His first book, *Transit of Venus* (1992), has been called 'probably the best modern travelogue about the Pacific'. More recently his biography of the writer Norman Lewis, *Semi-Invisible Man* (2008), has been received with widespread critical acclaim. He has written for many publications including the *Guardian* and the *New Statesman*, and presented radio and television documentaries on writers including Robert Louis Stevenson, F. Scott Fitzgerald and José Saramago. He lives in south-west England.

## HESPERUS PRESS

Hesperus Press is committed to bringing near what is far – far both in space and time. Works written by the greatest authors, and unjustly neglected or simply little known in the English-speaking world, are made accessible through new translations and a completely fresh editorial approach. Through these classic works, the reader is introduced to the greatest writers from all times and all cultures.

For more information on Hesperus Press, please visit our website: **www.hesperuspress.com**

# SELECTED TITLES FROM HESPERUS PRESS

ML          1/12